Bill o'th' Hoylus End

Revised Edition of Poems

Bill o'th' Hoylus End

Revised Edition of Poems

ISBN/EAN: 9783337206512

Printed in Europe, USA, Canada, Australia, Japan

Cover: Foto ©Andreas Hilbeck / pixelio.de

More available books at **www.hansebooks.com**

REVISED

EDITION OF POEMS

BY

Bill o'th' Hoylus End.

PRICE TWO SHILLINGS.

PRINTED AND PUBLISHED BY
JOHN OVEREND, COOK LANE, KEIGHLEY.
1891.

PREFACE.

The AUTHOR respectfully submits to the general public of his native town and district, this volume of poems, containing some of the chief results of his musings for the past thirty years. He hopes that the volume, which is in reality the production of a life-time, will in many ways be deemed worthy of the kind and courteous approbation of his numerous patrons and friends, as well as the indulgence of literary critics.

In launching forth the work, the Author begs to tender to his patrons and the public generally, his most sincere and hearty thanks for the assistance they have ever rendered him so as to enable him to acquire the necessary leisure for the cultivation of his muse. The result now achieved is not the comprehensive collection of the efforts of the author, but it may be taken as a selection and a representation of his more generally interesting productions from time to time.

Various reasons have operated in the time of the publication and the curtailment of this volume; but it is now submitted with every respect to the public for their perusal. Many of his poems, which are not found in the present volume, the author trusts will be deemed worthy of being treasured in the scrap books of his friends. Of the literary merits of the composition, it would ill become the author in any way to descant upon; but in regard to these he leaves himself entirely and absolutely in the hands of a critical, and, he hopes, an indulgent public, feeling assured that he may trust himself in the hands of his readers.

No formal dedication is here made to any particular patron, but the book is submitted without the powerful influence of any conspicuous name or the commendation of any well-known literary friend; and like Dr. Johnson of old, failing patrons, he trusts that his work will, in the midst of his numerous competitors, locally and generally, be thought worthy of the attention of the various classes of the public.

AUGUST, 1891.

CONTENTS.

CONTENTS—*Continued.*

The Grand Old Man of Oakworth.

COME, hand me down that rustic harp,
　　From off that rugged wall,
For I must sing another song
　　To suit the Muse's call,
For she is bent to sing a pæan,
　　On this eventful year,
In praise of the philanthropist
　　Whom all his friends hold dear—
　　　　The Grand Old Man of Oakworth,
　　　　Beyond his eightieth year!

No flattery! My honest Muse,
　　Nor yet be thou servile;
But tinkle up that harp again,
　　A moment to beguile.
Altho' the bard be rude and rough,
　　Yet, he is ever proud
To do the mite that he can do,
　　And thus proclaim aloud—
　　　　The Grand Old Man of Oakworth,
　　　　Of whom we all are proud!

For base indeed were any bard
　　That ever sang on earth,
Did he not wish his neighbour well,
　　And praise his sterling worth.

Leave state affairs and office
  To those of younger blood,
But I am with the patriot,
  The noble, wise, and good—
    The Grand Old Man of Oakworth,
    The wise, the great, the good !

This worthy old philanthropist,
  Whom all his neighbours greet ;
Who has a smile for every one
  Whom he may chance to meet—
Go to yon pleasant village,
  On the margin of the moor,
And you will hear his praises sung
  By all the aged poor—
    The Grand Old Man of Oakworth,
    A friend unto the poor !

Long may he live ! and happy be,
  The patriot and the sire ;
And may some other harp give praise,
  Whose notes will sound much higher.
His thirst for knowledge, worth, and lore—
  His heart was ever there—
This worthy old philanthropist,
  Beyond his eightieth year !—
    The Grand Old Man of Oakworth,
    Beyond his eightieth year.

THOUGHTS SUGGESTED

Dr. Dobie's Lecture on Burns.

THOUGH murky are the days and short,
　　And man he finds but little sport,
　　　These gloomy days, to cheer him ;
Yet, if a Dobie should, perchance,
Come out before an audience,
　　　'Tis worth our while to hear him.

Right pleased was I, dear sir, to hear
Your lecture on that subject dear,
　　　So grand and superhuman ;
For all the world doth pay regard
To Bobbie Burns, the Scottish bard,
　　　The patriot and the ploughman.

Your words, indeed, were passing good,
On him who kenned and understood
　　　The kirk and all its ranting ;
Who "held the mirror" up, indeed,
To show the "muckle unco-guid"
　　　Their double-dyéd canting.

You painted him sometimes in glee
While other times in poverty—
　　　To gold without alliance ;
Yet, after all he kept his pace,
And looked grim fortune in the face,
　　　And set him at defiance.

But, alas! the picture, was it true?
Of Burns' parents, poor and low—
   So furrowed and so hoary—
It makes our very hearts to burn
To think that "man was made to mourn,"
   And tell the sad, sad story.

You brought me back to days bygone,
When glad its banks I strolled upon,
   The river Doon so bonnie;
The roofless kirk and yard so green,
Where many a tombstone may be seen,
   With Tam and Souter Johnnie.

And when ye spake of yond bright star
That lingers in the lift afar,
   Where Burns was never weary
Of gazing on the far-off sphere,
Where dwells his angel lassie dear—
   His ain sweet Highland Mary!

But here my Muse its wings may lower;
Such flights are far beyond its power;
   So I will stop the jingle.
Sir, I am much obliged to you,
And I am much indebted to
   The Choir and Mr. Pringle.

What Profits Me.

W HAT profits me tho' I sud be
    The lord o' yonder castle gay ;
Hev rooms in state to imitate
    The princely splendour of the day
For what are all my carvéd doors,
My chandeliers or carpet floors,
    No art could save me from the grave.

What profits me tho' I sud be
    Decked i' costly costumes grand,
Like the Persian king o' kings,
    Wi' diamond rings to deck my hand :
For what wor all my grand attire,
That fooils both envy and admire,
    No gems could save me from the grave.

What profits me tho' I sud be
    Thy worthy host, O millionaire,
Hev cent. for cent. for money lent ;
    My wealth increasing ivvery year.
For what wor all my wealth to me,
Compared to immortality,
    Wealth could not save me from the grave.

What profits me tho' I sud be
    Even the gert Persian Shah,
My subjects stand at my command,
    Wi' fearful aspect and wi' awe ;
For what wor a despotic rule,
Wi' all the world at my control,
    All could not save me from the grave.

The Death of Gordon.

FROM the red fields of gore, 'midst war's dreadful
        clang,
  I hear a sad strain o'er oceans afar :
Oh, shame, shame upon you, ye proud men of England,
    Whose highest ambition is rapine and war !
            Through your vain wickedness
                Thousands are fatherless,
False your pretensions old Egypt to save ;
                Arabs with spear in hand
                Far in a distant land
Made our brave Gordon a sad and red grave.

On Nile's sunny banks, with the Arab's great nation,
    Brave Gordon was honoured and worshipped by all,
The acknowledged master of the great situation,
    Until England's bondholders caused Egypt to fall.
                Another great blunder,
                Makes the world wonder,
Where is Britannia's sword, sceptre and shield ?
                War and disaster
                Come thicker and faster,
Oh, for the days of the Great Beaconsfield !

Oh, Great Beaconsfield ! the wise and the clever,
    When will thy place in our nation be filled ?
Britannia's shrill answer is never, oh never,
    My Beaconsfield's dead, and my Gordon is killed !

Oh, blame not my foemen
Or a Brutus-like Roman,
Or Soudanese Arabs for Gordon's sad doom ;
But blame that vain Briton
Whose name is true written,
The slayer of Gordon, who fell at Khartoum.

The Earl of Beaconsfield.

I SING no song of superstition,
  No dark deeds of an Inquisition,
No mad-brain'd theme of wild ambition,
          For lo, their doom is sealed !
But I will use my best endeavour,
To praise the good, the wise, the clever,
Who will remember'd be for ever,
          The Earl of Beaconsfield.

When England was without alliance,
He bid the Russians bold defiance,
On Austria had no reliance
          In either flood or field ;
He proudly sent to Hornby message,
The Dardanelles ! go force the passage
In spite of Turkey, Bear, or Sausage,
          The dauntless Beaconsfield !

At Berlin, he with admiration
Was gazed upon by every nation,
And, master of the situation,
   Vow'd Britons ne'er would yield.
For I am here, you may depend on't,
This Eastern brawl to make an end on't,
To show both plaintiff and defendant
   I'm Earl of Beaconsfield !

Britannia now doth weep and ponder,
Bereaved of him, her child of wonder,
No earthly power could break asunder
   His love for England's weal.
And now those locks once dark as raven
(For laurel leaves ne'er deck'd a craven)
Wear a laurel crown in Heaven,
   Glorious Beaconsfield !

Come, Nivver Dee i' Thi Shell.

——o——

"COME, nivver dee i' thi shell, owd lad,"
  Are words but rudely said ;
Though they may cheer some stricken heart,
  Or raise some wretched head ;
For they are words I love mysel,
  They're music to my ear ;
They muster up fresh energy
  An' chase each doubt an' fear.

Nivver dee i' thi shell, owd lad,
  Though tha be poor indeed ;
Ner lippen ta long i' th' turnin' up
  Sa mich ov a friend in need ;
Fur few ther are, an' far between,
  That help a poor man thru ;
An' God helps them at help therseln,
  An' they hev friends enew.

Nivver dee i' thi shell, owd lad,
  Whativver thi creditors say ;
Tell um at least tha'rt foarst ta owe,
  If tha artant able ta pay ;
An' if they nail thi bits o' traps,
  An' sell tha dish an' spooin ;
Remember fickle forten lad,
  Shoo changes like the mooin.

Nivver dee i' thi shell, owd lad,
    Though some may laugh an' scorn ;
There wor nivver a neet afore ta neet,
    Bud what ther' com a morn ;
An' if blind forten used tha bad,
    Sho's happen noan so meean ;
Ta morn al come, an' then fer some
    The sun will shine ageean.

Nivver dee i' thi shell, owd lad,
    Bud let thi motto be,—
"Onward !" an' "Excelsior ;"
    An' try for t' top o't' tree :
An' if thi enemies still pursue,
    Which ten-ta-one they will,
Show um owd lad, tha'rt doin' weel,
    An' climin' up the hill.

Owd Betty's Advice.

——o——

SO Mary, lass, tha'rt bahn to wed
    It mornin', we young Blacksmith Ned,
An' though it maks thi mother sad,
        It's like to be ;
I've nowt ageean yond dacent lad,
        No more ner thee.

Bud let me tell tha what ta due,
For my advise might help tha thru ;
Be kind, and to thi husband true,
        An' I'll be bun
Tha'll nivver hev a day ta rue
        For owt tha's done.

Nah, try to keep thi former knack,
An' du thi weshin' in a crack,
Bud don't be flaid to bend thi back,
    Tha'll nobbut sweeat ;
So try an' hev a bit o' tack,
    An' du it neeat.

Be sure tha keeps fra bein' a flirt,
An' pride thysel i' bein' alert,—
An' mind ta mend thi husband's shirt,
    An' keep it cleean ;
It wod thi poor owd mother hurt,
    If tha wur meean.

Don't kal abaht like monny a wun,
Then hev to broil, an' sweeat, an' run ;
Bud alus hev thi dinner done
    Withaht a mooild ;
If it's nobbut meil, lass, set it on,
    An' hev it boiled.

Now Mary, I've no more ta say—
Tha gets thi choice an' tak thi way ;
An' if tha leets to rue, I pray,
    Don't blame thi mother :
I wish yeh monny a happy day
    Wi wun another.

T'owd Blacksmith's Advice ta his Son Ned.

— o —

S O, Ned, awm geen ta understand,
    Tha'rt bahn ta join i' wedlock band,
Ta travil thru life's weeary strand,
               Yond lass an' thee;
But if yer joinin' heart an' hand,
               It pleases me.

Nah tha'll hev trubbles, Ned, ta bear,
While pushin' thru this world o' care,
An' wat tha'll hev it face ta stare,
               It's hard ta tell;
Life's ups and dahns tha'll get ta share,
               So pleas thisel'.

Tha'rt weel an' strong, long may it last;
But age an' care creep on us fast;
Then act az tha can luke at t'past
               An' feel no shaam;
Then if tha'rt poor az sum ahteast,
               Tha'rt noan ta blame.

Doant sport abaht an' wagers bet,
But mind an' shun that foolish set
At cannut mak ther awn ta fet,
               Though shaam to say it.
An' mind tha keeps fra bein' i' debt,
               An' tha'll be reight.

Nah stick fast hod o' iron will ;
Push boldly on an' feear no ill ;
Keep Him i' veiw, whoa's mercies fill
The wurld sa wide.
No daht but His omnishent skill
Al be thi guide.

So Ned, mi lad, tak this advice,
Prove worthy o' yond lass's choice,
I' years ta cum tha may rejoice
Tha tuke her hand ;
An' listened ta thi father's voice,
An' his command.

Th' Furst Pair o' Briches.

—o—

AW remember the days o' mi bell-button jacket,
   Wi' its little lappels hangin' down ower mi waist,
An' mi grand bellosed cap,—noan nicer I'll back it,—
   Fer her at hed bowt it wur noan withaht taste ;
Fer shoo wur mi mother an' I wur her darling,
   An often shoo vowed it, an' stroked dahn mi hair,
An' shoo tuke ma to see her relashuns i' Harden
   It furst Pair o' Briches at ivver aw ware.

Aw remember the time when Aunt Betty an' Alice
   Sent fer me up to lewk at mi cloas,
An aw wauked up as prahd as a Frenchman fra Calais,
   Wi' mi tassel at t'side—i' mi jacket a rose.
Aw sooin saw mi uncles, both Johnny an' Willy,
   They both gav me pennies, an' off aw did steer :
But aw heeard um say this, "He's a fine lad is Billy,"
   It furst Pair o' Briches at ivver aw ware.

Aw remember t' time at ahr Robin and Johnny
　　Wur keeping their hens an' ducks i' t' yard,
Tha wur gamecocks an' bantams, wi' toppins so bonny,
　　An' noan on um mine—aw thowt it wur hard.
But aw saved up mi pennies aw gat fer mail pickin',
　　An' sooin gat a shilling by saving it fair,
Aw then became maister at least o' wun chicken,
　　It furst Pair o' Briches at ivver aw ware.

Aw remember wun Sabbath, an' t'sun it wor shining,
　　Aw went wi' mi father ta Hainworth ta sing ;
An' t'stage wur hung raand wi' bottle-green lining ;
　　And childer i' white made t' village ta ring.
We went ta owd Meshach's that day ta wur drinkin',
　　Though poor, tha wur plenty, an' summat ta spare ;
Says Meshach, "That lad, Jim, is just thee, aw'm thinking,
　　It furst Pair o' Briches at ivver tha ware."

Now them wur the days o' grim boggards and witches,
　　When Will-o'-the-wisp cud be seen in the swamp,
But nah are the days o' cheating fer riches,
　　An' a poor honest man is classed wi' a scamp.
Yes, them wur the days at mi mind worrant weary ;
　　O them wur the days aw knew no despair ;
O give me the time o' the boggard an' fairy,
　　Wi' t' furst Pair o' Briches at ivver aw ware.

Ah ! them wur the days aw sall allus remember,
　　Sud aw just as owd as Mathusalah last ;
Them wur mi March days, but nah it's September :
　　Ne'er to return again—them days are past.
But a time aw remember aboon onny other,
　　Aw kneeled o' mi knees an' sed the Lord's Prayer ;
Aw sed "God bless mi father, an' God bless mi mother,"
　　It furst Pair o' Briches at ivver aw ware.

O Welcome, Lovely Summer.

——o——

O WELCOME, lovely summer,
  Wi' thi golden days so long,
When the throstle and the blackbird
  Do charm us wi' ther song;
When the lark in early morning
  Takes his aerial flight;
An' the humming bat an' buzzard
  Frolic in the night.

O! welcome, lovely summer,
  With her rainbow's lovely form;
Her thunner an' her leetnin',
  An' her grandeur in the storm:
With her sunshine an' her shower,
  An' her whirlin' of the dust,
An' the maiden with her flagon,
  To sleck the mower's thirst.

O! welcome, lovely summer,
  When the woods wi' music ring,
An' the bees so heavy laden,
  To their hives their treasures bring:
When we seek some shady bower,
  Or some lovely little dell,
Or, bivock in the sunshine,
  Besides some cooling well.

O! welcome, lovely summer,
  With her roses in full bloom;
When the cowslaps an' the laalek
  Deck the cottage home;

When the cherry an' the berry
Give a grandeur to the charm ;
And the clover and the haycock
Scent the little farm.

O ! welcome, lovely summer,
Wi' the partridge on the wing ;
When the tewit an' the moorgam,
Up fra the heather spring,
From the crowber an' the billber,
An' the bracken an' the whin ;
As from the noisy tadpole,
We hear the crackin' din.
O ! welcome, lovely summer.

Burns's Centenary.

——o——

GO bring that tuther whisky in,
An' put no watter to it ;
Fur I mun drink a bumper off,
To Scotland's darlin' poet.

It's just one hunderd year to-day,
This Jenewarry morn,
Sin' in a lowly cot i' Kyle,
A rustic bard wur born.

He kittled up his muirland harp,
To ivvery rustic scene ;
An' sung the ways o' honest men,
His Davey an' his Jean.

There wur nivver a bonny flaar that grew
    Bud what he could admire ;
There wur nivver lovely hill or dale
    That suited not his lyre.

At last owd Coilia sed enough,
    Mi bardy thah did sing,
Then gently tuke his muirland harp,
    And brack it ivvery string.

An' bindin' up the holly wreath,
    Wi' all its berries red,
Shoo placed it on his noble brow,
    An' pensively shoo said :—

"So long as Willies brew ther malt,
    An' Robs and Allans spree ;
Mi Burns's songs an' Burns's name,
    Remember'd they shall be."

Waiting for t' Angels.

———o———

LIGGING here decad, mi poor Ann Lavina,
    Ligging alone, mi own darling child,
Just thi white hands crost on thi bosom,
Wi' features so tranquil, so calm, and so mild.

Ligging here decad, so white an' so bonny,
Hidding them eyes that oft gazed on mine ;
Asking for summat withaht ever speaking,
Asking thi father to say tha wur fine.

Ligging here decad, the child that so lov'd me,
At fane wod ha' hidden mi faults if shoo could ;
Wal thi wretch of a father despairin' stands ower tha,
Wal remorse and frenzy are freezin' his blood.

Ligging here deead, i' thi shroud an thi coffin,
Ligging alone in this poor wretched room ;
Just thi white hands crossed ower thi bosom,
Waiting for t'angels to carry tha home.

The Lass o' Newsholme Dean.

—o—

[Having spent the whole of the afternoon in this
romantic little glen, indulging in pleasant meditations,
I began to wend my way down the craggy pass that
leads to the bonny little hamlet of Goose Eye, and
turning round to take a last glance at this enchanting
vale—with its running whimpering stream—I beheld the
" Lass o' Newsholme Dean."   She was engaged in
driving home a Cochin China hen and her chickens.
Instantaneously I was seized with a poetic fit, and
gazing upon her as did Robert Tannyhill upon his
imaginary beauty, " The Flower of Dumblane," I
struck my lyre, and, although the theme of my song
turned out afterwards to be a respectable old woman
of 70 winters, yet there is still a charm in my " Lass
o' Newsholme Dean."]

THY kiss is sweet, thy words are kind,
    Thy love is all to me ;
Aw couldn't in a palace finé
    A lass more true ner thee :
An' if aw wor the Persian Shah,
    An' thee mi Lovely Queen,
The grandest diamond i' mi Crown
    Wor t' Lass o' Newsholme Dean.

The lady gay may heed tha not,
  An' passing by may sneer ;
The upstart squire's dowters laugh,
  When thou, my love, art near ;
But if all ther shinin' soverins
  War wared o' sattens green,
They mightn't be as handsome then
  As t' Lass o' Newsholme Dean.

When yellow autumn's lustre shines,
  An' hangs her golden ear,
An' nature's voice fra every bush
  Is singing sweet and clear,
'Neath some white thorn to song unknown,
  To mortal never seen,
'Tis there with thee I fain wad be,
  Mi Lass o' Newsholme Dean.

Od drat, who cares fur kings or queens,
  Mix'd in a nation's broil,
They nivver benefit the poor—
  The poor mun ollas toil.
An' thou gilded spectre, royalty,
  That dazzles folks's een,
Is nowt to me when I'm wi thee,
  Sweet Lass o' Newsholme Dean.

High fra the summit o' yon' crag,
  I view yon' smooky town,
Where forten she has deigned to smile
  On monny a simple clown :
Though free fra want, they're free fra brains ;
  An' yet no happier I ween,
Than this old farmer's wife an' hens,
  Aw saw i' Newsholme Dean.

The Broken Pitcher.

— o —

[The happiest moments of a soldier in times of peace
are when sat round the hearth of his neat little barrack
room, along with his comrades, spinning yarns and
telling tales; sometimes giving the history of some
famous battle or engagement in which he took a
prominent part; other times he will relate his own love
adventures; then the favourite of the room will oblige
them with his song of "Nelson" or "Napoleon"
(generally being the favourites with them);—then there
is the fancy tale teller, who amuses all.   But in all
cases the teller of a tale, yarn, or story, makes himself
the hero of it, and especially when he speaks of the
lass he left behind him; hence this adventure with the
"Lassie by the Well."]

THERE was a bonny Lassie once
　　Sitting by a well—
But what this bonny Lassie thought
　　I cannot, cannot tell—
When by there went a cavalier
　　Well known as Willie Wright,
Just in full marching order,
　　His armour shining bright.

" Ah maiden, lovely maiden, why
　　Sits thou by the spring?
Dost thou seek a lover, with
　　A golden wedding ring?
Or wherefore dost thou gaze on me,
　　With eyes so bright and wide?
Or wherefore does that pitcher lay
　　Broken by thy side?"

"My pitcher it is broken, sir,
  And this the reason is,
A villian came behind me,
  An' he tried to steal a kiss.
I could na take his nonsense,
  So ne'er a word I spoke,
But hit him with my pitcher,
  And thus you see 'tis broke."

"My uncle Jock McNeil, ye ken
  Now waits for me to come:
He canna mak his Crowdy,
  Till t'watter it goes home.
I canna tak him watter,
  And that I ken full weel,
And so I'm sure to catch it,—
  For he'll play the varry de'il."

"Ah maiden, lovely maiden,
  I pray be ruled by me;
Smile with thine eyes and ruby lips,
  And give me kisses three.
And we'll suppose my helmet is
  A pitcher made o' steel,
And we'll carry home some watter
  To thy uncle Jock McNeil."

She silently consented, for
  She blink'd her bonny ee,
I threw mi arms around her,
  And gave her kisses three.
To wrong the bonny Lassie
  I sware 'twould be a sin;
So knelt dahn by the watter
  To dip mi helmet in.

Out spake this bonny Lassie,
  "My soldier lad, forbear,
I wadna spoil thi bonny plume
  That decks thi raven hair;
Come buckle up thy sword again,
  Put on thi cap o' steel,
I carena for my pitcher, nor
  My uncle Jock McNeil."

I often think, my comrades,
  About this Northern queen,
And fancy that I see her smile,
  Though mountains lay between.
But should you meet her Uncle Jock,
  I hope you'll never tell
How I squared the broken pitcher,
  With the Lassie at the well.

Ode to Sir Titus Salt.

G O, string once more old Ebor's harp,
    And bring it here to me,
For I must sing another song,
  The theme of which shall be,—
A worthy old philanthropist,
  Whose soul in goodness soars,
And one whose name will stand as firm
  As rocks that gird our shores;
The fine old Bradford gentleman,
  The good Sir Titus Salt.

Heedless of others; some there are,
   Who all their days employ
To raise themselves, no matter how,
   And better men destroy :
How different is the mind of him,
   Whose deeds themselves are told,
Who values worth more nobly far
   Than all the heaps of gold.

His feast and revels are not such,
   As those we hear and see,
No princely show does he indulge,
   Nor feats of revelry ;
But in the orphan schools they are,
   Or in the cot with her,
The widow and the orphan of
   The shipwrecked mariner,

When stricken down with age and care,
   His good old neighbours grieved,
Or loss of family or mate,
   Or all on earth bereaved ;
Go see them in their houses,
   Where peace their days may end,
And learn from them the name of him
   Who is their aged friend.

With good and great his worth shall live,
   With high or lowly born ;
His name is on the scroll of fame,
   Sweet as the songs of morn ;
While tyranny and villany
   Is surely stamped with shame ;
A nation gives her patriot
   A never-dying fame.

No empty titles ever could
   His principles subdue,
His queen and country too he loved,—
   Was loyal and was true :
He craved no boon from royalty,
   Nor wished their pomp to share,
Far nobler is the soul of him,
   The founder of Saltaire.

Thus lives this sage philanthropist,
   From courtly pomp removed,
But not secluded from his friends,
   For frienship's bond he loved;
A noble reputation too
   Crowns all his latter days ;
The young men they admire him,
   And the aged they him praise.

Long life to thee, Sir Titus,
   The darling of our town ;
Around thy head while living,
   We'll weave a laurel crown.
Thy monument in marble
   May suit the passer by,
But a monument in all our hearts
   Will never, never die.

And when thy days are over,
   And we miss thee on our isle,
Around thy tomb for ever
   May unfading laurels smile :
Then may the sweetest flowers
   Usher in the spring ;
And roses in the gentle gales,
   Their balmy odours fling.

May summer's beams shine sweetly,
   Upon thy hallowed clay,
And yellow autumn o'er thy head,
   Yield many a placid ray ;
May winter winds blow slightly,—
   The green-grass softly wave,
And falling snow drop lightly
   Upon thy honoured grave.

Cowd az Leead.

A N' arta fra thi father torn,
   So early i' thi youthful morn,
An' mun aw pine away forlorn,
       I' grief an' pain?
Fer consolashun I sall scorn
       If tha be ta'en.

O yes, tha art, an' aw mun wail
Thi loss through ivvery hill an' dale,
Fer nah it is too true a tale,
       Tha'rt cowd az leead.
An' nah thi bonny face iz pale,
       Tha'rt deead! tha'rt deead!

Aw's miss tha when aw cum fra t'shop,
An' see thi bat, an' ball, an' top ;
An' aw's be ommust fit ta drop,
       Aw sall so freeat,
An' Oh! mi varry heart may stop
       An' cease to beeat !

Ah'd allus aimed, if tha'd been spar'd,
Of summat better to hev shared
Ner what thi poor owd father fared,
         I' this cowd sphere ;
Yet, after all, aw'st noan o' cared
         If tha'd stayed here.

But O ! Tha Conquerer Divine,
'At vanquished deeath i' Palestine,
Tak to Thi arms this lad o' mine
         Noan freely given ;
But mak him same as wun o' Thine,
         Wi' Thee i' Heaven.

The Factory Girl.

SHOO stud beside her looms an' watch'd
    The shuttle passin' through,
But yet her soul wur sumweer else,
  'Twor face ta face wi' Joe.
They saw her lips move as in speech,
  Yet none cud hear a word,
An' but for t'grindin' o' the wheels,
  This language might be heard.

" I't' spite o' all thi treacherous art,
  At length aw breeathe again ;
The pityin' stars hes tane mi part,
  An' eas'd a wretch's pain.
An' Oh ! aw feel as fra a maze,
  Mi rescued soul is free,
Aw knaw aw do not dream an daze
  I' fancied liberty.

"Extinguish'd nah is ivvery spark,
    No love for thee remains,
Fer heart-felt love i' vain sall strive
    Ta live, when tha disdains.
No longer when thi name I hear,
    Mi conscious colour flies !
No longer when thi face aw see,
    Mi heart's emotions rise.

"Catcht i' the bird-lime's treacherous twigs,
    Ta wheer he chonc'd ta stray,
The bird his fastened feathers leaves,
    Then gladly flies away.
His shatter'd wings he sooin renews,
    Of traps he is aware ;
Fer by experience he is wise,
    An' shuns each future snare.

"Awm speikin' nah, an' all mi aim
    Is but ta pleeas mi mind ;
An' yet aw care not if mi words
    Wi' thee can credit find.
Ner dew I care if my decease
    Sud be approved bi thee ;
Or whether tha wi' equal ease
    Does tawk ageean wi' me.

"But, yet, tha false deceivin' man,
    Tha's lost a heart sincere ;
Aw naw net which wants comfort mooast,
    Or which hes t'mooast ta fear.
But awm suer a lass more fond an' true
    No lad could ivver find :
But a lad like thee is easily fun—
    False, faithless, and unkind."

Bonny Lark.

SWEETEST warbler of the wood,
  Rise thy soft bewitching strain,
And in pleasure's sprightly mood,
    Soar again.

With the sun's returning beam,
  First appearance from the east,
Dimpling every limpid stream,
    Up from rest.

Thro' the airy mountains stray,
  Chant thy welcome songs above,
Full of sport and full of play,
    Songs of love.

When the evening cloud prevails,
  And the sun gives way for night,
When the shadows mark the vales,
    Return thy flight.

Like the cottar or the swain,
  Gentle shepherd, or the herd ;
Rest thou till the morn again,
    Bonny bird !

Like thee, on freedom's airy wing,
  May the poet's rapturous spark,
Hail the first approach of spring,
    Bonny lark !

Home of My Boyish Days.

HOME of my boyish days, how can I call
 Scenes to my memory, that did befall?
How can my trembling pen find power to tell
The grief I experienced in bidding farewell?
Can I forget the days joyously spent,
That flew on so rapidly, sweet with content?
Can I then quit thee, whose memory's so dear,
Home of my boyish days, without one tear?

Can I look back on happy days gone by,
Without one pleasant thought, without one sigh
Ah, no! though never more these eyes may dwell
On thee, old cottage home, I love so well:
Home of my childhood! wherever I be,
Thou art the nearest and dearest to me!

Can I forget the songs sung by my sire,
Like some prophetic bard tuning the lyre?
Sweet were the notes that he taught to the young;
Psalms for the Sabbath, on Sabbath were sung;
And the young minstrels enraptured would come
To the little lone cottage I once called my home.

Can I forget the dear landscape around,
Where in my boyish days I could be found,
Stringing my hazel-bow, roaming the wood,
Fancying myself to be bold Robin Hood?
Then would my mother say—"Where is he gone?
I'm waiting for shuttles that he should have 'wun'?"—
She in that cottage there, knitting her healds,
And I, her young forester, roaming the fields.

But the shades of the evening gather slowly around,
The twilight it thickens and darkens the ground,
Night's sombre mantle is spreading the plain.
And as I turn round to look on thee again,
To take one fond look, one last fond adieu,
By night's envious hand thou art snatched from my view;
But Oh! there's no darkness—to me—no decay,
Home of my boyhood, can chase thee away!

Ode ta Spring Sixty-four.

****

O WELCOME, young princess, thou sweetest of
   dowters,
  An' furst bloomin' issue o' King Sixty-four,
Wi' thi brah deck'd wi' gems o' the purest o' waters,
  Tha tells us thi sire, stern winter, is ower.

We hail thi approach wi' palm-spangled banners;
  The plant an' the saplin' await thi command;
An' Natur herseln, to show her good manners,
  Nah spreads her green mantle all ower the land.

Tha appears in t' orchard, in t' garden, an' t' grotto,
  Where sweet vegetation anon will adorn;
Tha smiles on the lord no more than the cottar,
  For thi meanest o' subjects tha nivver did scorn.

O hasten ta labour! ye wise, O be goin'!
  These words they are borne on the wings o' the wind;
Tha bids us be early i' plewin' an' sowin',
  Fer him at neglects, tha'll leave him behind.

Address ta t' First Wesherwoman.

****

I' SOOTH shoo wor a reeal God-send,
 Ta t' human race the greatest friend,
An' liv'd, no daht, at t'other end
   O' history.
Her name is nah, yah may depend,
   A mystery.

But sprang shoo up fra royal blood,
Or some poor slave beyond the Flood,
Mi blessing on the sooap an' sud
   Shoo did invent ;
Her name sall renk among the good,
   If aw get sent.

If nobbut in a rainy dub,
Shoo did at furst begin ta skrub,
Or hed a proper weshin' tub—
   It's all the same ;
Aw'd give a crahn, if aw'd to sub,
   To get her name.

I' this wide world aw'm set afloat,
Th' poor regg'd possessor of one coat ;
Yet linen clean, aw on tha dote,
   An' thus assert,
Tha'rt worthy o' great Shakespeare's note—
   A clean lin' shirt.

Low is mi lot, an' hard mi ways,
While paddlin' thro' life's stormy days ;
Yet aw will sing t'owd lass's praise,
    Wi' famous glee ;
Tho' rude an' rough sud be mi lays,
    Shoo's t'lass for me.

Bards hev sung the fairest fair,
Their rosy cheeks an' auburn hair ;
The dying lover's deep despair,
    Their harps hev rung ;
But useful wimmin's songs are rare,
    An' seldom sung.

In a Pleasant Little Valley.

IN a pleasant little valley near the ancient town of
 Ayr,
Where the laddies they are honest, and the lassies they
 are fair ;
Where Doon in all her splendour ripples sweetly through
 the wood,
And on its banks not long ago a little cottage stood ;
'Twas there, in all her splendour, on a January morn,
Appeared old Coila's genius—when Robert Burns was
 born.

Her mantle large of greenish hue and robe of tartan
  shone,
And round its mystic border seen was Luger, Ayr,
  and Doon;
A leaf-clad holly bough was twined so graceful round
  her brow,
She was the darling native muse of Scotia then, as now:
So grand old Coila's genius on this January morn,
Appeared in all her splendour when Robert Burns was
  born.

She vowed she ne'er would leave him till he sung old
  Scotia's plains—
The daisy, and the milk-white thorn he tuned in
  lovely strains;
And sung of yellow autumn, or some lovely banks
  and braes:
And make each cottage home resound with his sweet
  tuneful lays,
And sing how Coila's genius, on a January morn,
Appeared in all her splendour when Robert Burns
  was born.

She could not teach him painting like her Cunningham
  at home,
Nor could she teach him sculpturing like Angelo of
  Rome;
But she taught him how to wander her lovely hills
  among,
And sing her bonny burns and glens in simple rustic
  song;
This old Coila's genius did that January morn,
Vow in all her splendour when Robert Burns was born.

And in the nights of winter, when stormy winds do roar,
And the fierce dashing waves are heard on Ayr's old
  craggy shore,
The young and old encircled around the cheerful fire,
Will talk of Rob the Ploughman and tune the
  Scottish lyre ;
And sing how Coila's genius on a January morn,
Appeared in all her splendour when Robert Burns
  was born.

John o'l' Bog an' Keighley Feffy Goast :

A TALE O' POVERTY.

"Some books are lies fra eud to end,
And some great lies were never penn'd ;
But this that I am gaun to tell,
∗ ∗ ∗ Lately on a night befel."—BURNS.

'TWOR twelve o'clock wun winter's neet,
  Net far fra Kersmas time,
When I met wee this Feffy Goast,
  The subject of mi rhyme.

I'd been hard up for monny a week,
  Mi way I cuddant see,
For trade an' commerce wor as bad
  As ivvor they could be.

T'poor haud-loom chaps wor running wild,
   An' t'combers wor quite sick,
Fer weeks they nivver pool'd a slip,
   Ner t'weivers wave a pick.

An' I belong'd ta t'latter lot,
   An' them wor t'war o't' two,
Fer I'd nine pair o' jaws i' t'haase,
   An nowt for 'em ta do.

T'owd wife at t' time wor sick i' bed,
   An' I'd a shockin' cowd,
Wal t'youngest barn we hed at home,
   Wor nobbut three days owd.

Distracted to mi varry heart,
   At sitch a bitter cup,
An' lippenin' ivvery day at com,
   At summat wod turn up ;

At last I started off wun neet,
   To see what I could mak ;
Determin'd I'd hev summat ta eit,
   Or else I'd noan go back.

Through t'Skantraps an' be t' Bracken Benk,
   I tuke wi' all mi meet ;
Be t' Wire Mill an' Ingrow Loin,
   Reight into t' oppen street.

Saint John's Church spire then I saw,
   An' I wor rare an' fain,
Fer near it stood t'owd parsonage—
   I cuddant be mistain.

So up I went ta t' Wicket Gate,
  Though sad I am ta say it,
Resolv'd to ax 'em for some breead,
  Or else some brocken meit.

Bud just as I wor shackin' it,
  A form raase up before,
An' sed " What does ta want, tha knave,
  Shackin' t' Wicket Door ? "

He gav me then ta understand,
  If I hedant come to pray,
At t'grace o' God an' t'breead o' life,
  Wor all they gav away.

It's fearful nice fer folk ta talk
  Abaat ther breead o' life,
An' specially when they've plenty,
  Fer t'childer an' ther wife.

Bud I set off ageean at t'run,
  For I weel understood,
If I gat owt fra that thear clahn,
  It woddant do ma good.

I' travellin' on I thowt I heeard,
  As I went nearer t'tahn,
A thaasand voices i' mi ears,
  Sayin' " John, whear are ta bahn ? "

In ivvery grocer's shop I pass'd,
  A play-card I could see,
I' t'biggest type at e'er wod print—
  " There's nowt here, lad, fer thee."

Wal ivvery butcher's shop I pass'd,
　　Asteead o' meit wor seen,
A mighty carvin'-knife hung up,
　　Reight fair afore mi een.

Destruction wor invitin' me,
　　I saw it fearful clear,
For ivvery druggist window sed—
　　" Real poison is sold here."

At last I gav a frantic howl,
　　A shaat o' dreead despair,
I seized missen by t'toppin then,
　　An' shack'd an' lugged mi hair.

Then quick as leetnin' ivver wor,
　　A thowt com i' mi heead—
I'd tak a walk to t'Simetry,
　　An' meditate wi' t'deead.

T'owd Church clock wor striking' t' time
　　At folk sud be asleep,
Save t'Bobbies at wor on ther beat,
　　An' t'Pindar after t'sheep.

Wi' lengthen'd pace I hasten'd off
　　At summat like a trot ;
Ta get ta t'place I started for,
　　Mi blood wor boiling hot.

An' what I saw at Lackock Gate,
　　Rear'd up ageean a post,
I cuddant tell—but yet I thowt
　　It wor another goast !

But whether it wor a goast or net,
   I heddant time ta luke,
Fer I wor takken bi surprise
   When turning t'Sharman's Nuke.

Abaat two hunderd yards i' t'front,
   As near as I could think,
I thowt I heeard a dreeadful noise,
   An' nah an' then a clink!

Whativver can these noises be?
   Some robbers, then I thowt!—
I'd better step aside an' see,
   They're happen up ta nowt!

So I gat ower a fence ther wor,
   An' peeping threw a gate,
Determin'd to be satisfied,
   If I'd a while to wait.

At last two figures com ta t'spot
   Whear I hed hid misel,
Then walkers'-earth and brimstone,
   Most horridly did smell.

Wun on em hed a nine-tail'd cat,
   His face as black as sooit,
His name, I think wor Nickey Ben,
   He hed a clovven fooit.

An' t'other wor all skin an' bone
   His name wor Mr. Deeath;
Withaat a stitch o' clooas he wor,
   An' seem'd quite aght o' breeath.

He hed a scythe, I plainly saw,
  He held it up aloft,
Just same as he wor bahn ta maw
  Owd Jack O'Doodle's Croft.

"Where are ta bahn ta neet, grim phiz?"
  Sed Nickey, wi' a grin,
"Tha knaws I am full up below,
  An' cannot tak more in."

"What is't ta thee?" said Spinnel Shanks,
  "Tha ruffin of a dog,
I'm nobbut bahn mi raands ageean,
  Ta see wun John o't' Bog.

"I cannot see it fer mi life,
  What it's ta dew wi' thee;
Go mind thi awn affairs, owd Nick,
  An' nivver thee heed me."

"It is my business, Spinnel Shanks,
  Whativver tha may say,
Fer I been rostin' t'human race
  Fer monny a weary day."

Just luke what wark, I've hed wi' thee,
  This last two yer or so;
Wi' Germany an Italy,
  An' even Mexico.

An' then tha knaws that Yankey broil
  Browt in some thaasands more;
An' sooin fra Abyssinia,
  They'll bring black Theodore.

" So drop that scythe, owd farren deeath,
  Let's rest a toathree wick ;
Fer what wi' t'seet o't' frying pan,
  Tha knows I'm ommost sick."

" I sall do nowt o't' sort," says Deeath,
  Who spack it wi' a grin,
I's' just do as I like fer thee,
  So tha can hod thi din."

This made owd Nick fair raging mad,
  An' liftin' up his whip,
He gav owd Spinnel Shanks a lash
  Across his upper lip.

Then like a neighin' steed, lean Shanks,
  To give owd Nick leg bail,
He started off towards the tahn,
  Wi' Nick hard on his trail.

Then helter-skelter off they went,
  As ower t'fence I lape ;
I thowt—well, if it matters owt,
  I've made a nice escape.

But nah the mooin began ta shine
  As breet as it could be ;
An dahn the vale of t'Aire I luked,
  Whear I could plainly see.

The trees wor deeadly pale wi' snaw,
  An' t'windin' Aire wor still,
An' all wor quite save t'hullats,
  At wor screamin' up o't' hill.

Owd Rivock End an' all araûnd
   Luk'd like some fiendish heead,
Fer t'more I star'd an' t'more I thowt
   It did resemble t'deead.

The Friendly Oaks wor alter'd nah,
   Ta what I'd seen afore ;
An' luk'd as though they'd nivver be
   T'owd Friendly Oaks no more.

Fer wun wor like a giant grim,
   His nooas com to a point,
An' wi' a voice like thunner sed—
   " The times are aught o't'joint !"

An' t'other, like a whippin'-post,
   Bud happen net as thin,
Sed " T' times el alter yet, owd fooil,
   So pray nah, hod thi din !"

I tuke no farther gawm o' them,
   But paddl'd on mi way ;
Fer when I ivver mak a vah,
   I stick ta what I say.

I heddant goan so far ageean,
   Afoar I heeard a voice,
Exclaiming—wi' a fearful groan—
   "Go mak a hoil i' t'ice !"

I turned ma rahnd wheer t'sahnd com fro,
   An' cautiously I bowed,
Sayin' " Thenk ye, Mr. Magic Voice,
   I'm flaid o' gettin' cowd."

But nah a sudden shack tuke place,
 A sudden change o' scene ;
Fer miles wheer all wor white afoar,
 Wor nah a bottle-green.

Then com a woman donn'd i' white,
 A mantle gert shoo wore ;
A nicer lukin', smarter form
 I nivver saw afoar.

Her featers did resemble wun
 O' that kind-hearted lot,
'At's ivver ready to relieve
 The poor man in his cot.

Benevolence wor strongly mark'd
 Upon her noble heead ;
An' on her bruhst ye might ha' read,
 "Who dees fer want o' breead ?"

In fact, a kinder-hearted soul
 Owd Yorkshire cuddant boast ;
An' who wod feel the least alarmed
 Ta talk ta sitch a ghoast ?

I didn't feel at all afraid,
 As nearer me shoo drew :
I sed — "Good evening, Mrs. Ghoast,
 Hahivver do ye dew ?"

Sho nivver seem'd to tak no gawm,
 Bud pointed up at t'mooin,
An' beckon'd me ta follow her
 Reight dahn bi t'Wattery Loin.

So on we went, an' dahn we turn'd,
　　An' nawther on us spak ;
Bud nah an' then shoo twined her heead,
　　Ta see if I'd runn'd back.

·At t'last sho stopped and turned arahnd,
　　An' luk'd ma fair i' t'een ;
'Twor nah I picked it aght at wunce,
　　Sho wor no human bein'.

Sho nave a paper fra her bruhst,
　　Like some long theatre bill ;
An' then shoo sed " Wake mortal,
　　Will ta read to me this will ?

" Bud first, afoar tha starts to read,
　　I'll tell thee who I is ;
Tha lukes a dacent chap eniff—
　　I judge it by thi phiz.

" Well, I've a job fer thee to do—
　　That is, if tha will do it ;
I think tha'rt t'likliest man I knaw,
　　Becos tha art a poet.

If I am not mistaen, mi friend,
　　I often hear thi name ;
I think they call tha John o' t'Bog ";—
　　Says I—" Owd lass, it's t'same."

" It's just so mony years this day,
　　I knaw it by mi birth,
Sin' I departed mortal life,
　　An' left this wicked earth.

" But ere I closed these een to go
   Into eternity,
I thowt I'd dew a noble act,
   A deed o' charity.

" I hed a bit o' brass, tha knaws,
   Some land an' property :
I thowt it might be useful, John,
   To folks i' poverty.

" So then I made a will o't' lot,
   Fer that did suit mi mind ;
I planned it as I thowt wor t'best,
   To benefit mankind.

" I left a lot ta t' Grammar Skooil ;
   By reading t'will tha'll see,
That ivvery body's barn, tha knaws,
   May hev ther skooilin' free.

" An' if tha be teetotal, John—
   Tha may think it a fault—
To ivvery woman liggin' in
   I gav a peck o' malt.

" Bud t'biggest bulk o' brass 'at's left,
   As tha'll hev heeard afoear,
Wor to be dealt half-yearly
   Among ahr Keighley poor

" I certainly did mak a flaw,
   Fer which I've rued, alas !
'Twor them 'at troubled t'parish, John,
   Sud hev no Feffee Brass.

"An' nah, if tha will be so kind,
　　Go let mi trustees knaw
'At I sall be oblidg'd to them
　　To null that little flaw.

"An' will ta menshun this an' all,
　　Wal tha's an interview?—
Tell 'em to share t'moast brass to t'poor,
　　Whativver else they do.

"Then I sall rest an' be at peace,
　　Both here an' when i' Heaven;
When them 'at need it will rejoice
　　Fer t'bit o' brass I've given;

"An' tell 'em to remember thee
　　Upon t'next Feffee Day!"
I says—"I sallant get a meg,
　　I'm gettin' parish pay."

So when shoo'd spokken what shoo thowt,
　　An' tell'd me what to do,
I ax'd her if shoo'd harken me,
　　Wal I just said a word or two.

"I'll nut tell you one word o' lie,
　　As sure as my name's John;
I think at you are quite i' t'mist
　　Abaht things going on.

"Folks gether in fra far an' near,
　　When it is Feffee Day,
An' think they hev another lowse,
　　Wi' t'little bit o' pay.

"Astead o' givin' t'brass to t'poor,
  It's shocking fer to tell,
They'll hardly let 'em into t'door—
  I knaw it bi misell.

"Astead o' bein' a peck o' malt
  Fer t'wimmen liggin' in,
It's geen to rascals ower-grown,
  To drink i' rum an' gin.

"Then them at is—I understand—
  What you may call trustees;
They hev ther favourites, you knaw,
  An' gives to who they please.

"Some's nowt to do but shew ther face,
  An' skrew ther maath awry;
An' t'brass is shuvv'd into ther hand,
  As they are passin' by.

"There's monny a woman I knaw weel,
  Boath middle-aged and owd,
'At's waited fer ther bit o' brass,
  An' catch'd ther deeath o' cowd;

"Wol mony a knave wi' lots o' brass
  Hes cum i' all his pride,
An' t'flunkeys, fer to let him pass,
  Hes push'd t'poor folk aside.

"Fra Bradford, Leeds, an' Halifax,
  If they've a claim, they come;
But what wi' t'railway fares an' drink,
  It's done bi they get hooam.

"Wol mony a poorer family
  'At's nut been named i' t'list,
Reight weel desarves a share o' t'spoil,
  But, thenk ye, they are miss'd.

"We see a man at hes a haase,
  Or happen two or three,
They 'Mister' him, an' hand him aght
  Five times as mitch as me.

" 'Twor better if yo'd teed yer brass
  Tight up i' sum owd seck,
An' getten t'Corporation brooms,
  To sweep it into t'beck."

No longer like Capia's form,
  Wi' a tear i' both her een,
But like the gallant Camilla,
  The Volscian warrior Queen.

Shoo, kneelin', pointed up aboon,
  An' vah'd, be all so breet,
Sho'd wreak her vengence on ther heeads,
  Or watch 'em day an' neet.

Shoo call'd the Furies to her aid,
  An' Diræ's names shoo used,
An' sware if I hed spocken t'truth,
  Shoo hed been sore abus'd.

"Alas, poor Ghoast!"—I sed to her—
  "Indeed, it is too true";
Wi' that sho vanish'd aght o' t'seet,
  Sayin' "Johnny lad, adieu!"

In Memory of
THOMAS IRELAND,

Police Superintendent, Keighley.

BORN 1821. DIED 1867.

"He was a man, take him for all-in-all, we shall not look upon his
like again?"—SHAKSPEARE.

WHO knew his virtues must his death deplore
    And long lament that Ireland is no more ;
Set is the sun that shone with all its rays,
And claimed from every one their warmest praise.

Mute are those lips, whose mildest accents spoke
Their sterling worth, down to the harmless joke ;
Clear-seeing his soul, for lo! that mind was one
That envied nothing underneath the sun.

To speak the truth, he never was afraid ;
His country's weal, his country's laws obeyed :
A pensive calm reigned on his noble brow,
While in his eye you read the solemn vow :—

" I harm no one ; no one will I betray ;
My duty is to watch and see fair play ;
My friendship is to no one set confined ;
My heart and hand are given to all mankind."

Oh ancient town of legendary strain
When will his place in thee be filled again !
For men like he, possessed of sterling worth,
Are few and far between upon the earth

Such was the man the weeping mourners mourn,
Lost to his friends, ah ! never to return ;
Fled to the spheres where he in peace must dwell,
While all who knew him bid a long farewell.

A Yorkshireman's Christmas.

AW hev ten or twelve pund o' gooid meit,
   A small cheese an' a barrel o' beer ;
Aw'll welcome King Kersmas to neet,
   For he nobbut comes once in a year.

Send ahr Will dahn ta Tommy Spoyle Wood's,
   An' tell him ta send up a log ;
An' tell him an' Betty to come,
   For Tommy's a jolly owd dog.

Aw mean ta forget all my debts,
   An' aw mean ta harbour no grief ;
Nobbut emptying glasses an' plates
   O' their contents o' beer an' gooid beef.

Them barns they care nowt abaht drink,
   Like us 'at's advanced into years ;
So Sally, lass, what does ta think,
   If ta buys 'em some apples an' pears ?

Ahr David's a fine little lad,
   An' ahr Nancy's a fine little lass ;
When aw see 'em aw do feel so glad,
   So bring me a quart an' a glass !

Come, Sally, an' sit bi mi side,
   We've hed both wur ups an' wur dahns ;
Awm fane at aw made thee mi bride,
   An' awm prahd o' both thee an' wur barns.

We're as happy as them 'at's more brass,
   In a festival holly-decked hall ;
We envy no mortal, owd lass ;
   Here's peace an' good-will unto all !

An' may ev'ry poor crater to neet,
   If nivver before in his life,
Hev plenty to drink an' to eyt,
   Fer both him, an' his barns, an' his wife.

Lines on the Late
MR. THOMAS CRAVEN.

DARKNESS his curtain, and his bed the dust—
   The friend we had but yesterday;
His spirit to the unknown land
                  Hath fled away.

Ah! death's strong key hath turned the lock,
   And closed again its ponderous door,
That ne'er for him shall ope again—
                  Ah, nevermore!

Now pity swells the tide of love,
   And rolls through all our bosoms deep,
For we have lost a friend indeed;
                  And thus we weep.

'Twas his to learn in Nature's school
   To love his fellow-creatures dear;
His bounty fed the starving poor
                  From year to year.

But thou, pale moon, unclouded beam,
   And O! ye stars, shine doubly bright,
And light him safe across the lake
                  To endless light!

Gooise an' Giblet Pie.

A KERSMAS song I'll sing, mi lads,
  If ye'll bud hearken me;
An incident i' Kersmas time,
  I' eighteen sixty-three;
Whithaht a stypher i' the world—
  I'd scorn to tell a lie—
I dinéd wi a gentleman
  O' gooise an' giblet pie.

I've been i' lots o' feeds, mi lads,
  An' hed some rare tucks-aght;
Blood-puddin days with killin' pigs,
  Minch pies an' thumpin' tarts;
But I wired in, an' reight an' all,
  An' supp'd when I wor dry,
Fer I wor dinin' wi' a gentleman
  O' gooise an' giblet pie.

I hardly knew what ail'd ma, lads,
  I felt so fearful prahd;
Mi ears pricked up, mi collar rahse,
  T'ards a hawf-a-yard;
Mi chest stood aght, mi charley in,
  Like horns stuck aght mi tie;
Fer I dinéd wi' a gentleman
  O' gooise an' giblet pie.

I often think o' t'feed, mi lads,
  When t' gentleman I meet;
Bud nauther on us speiks a word
  Abaht that glorious neet;
In fact, I hardly can misel,
  I feel so fearful shy;
Fer I ate a deal o' t'rosted gooise,
  An' warm'd his giblet pie.

The Grand Old Man.

I SING of a statesman, a statesman of worth,
The grandest old statesman there is upon earth;
When his axe is well sharpened we all must agree,
He can level a nation as well as a tree.

He can trundle such words from his serpent-like tongue
As fairly bewilder both old men and young;
He can make some believe that's black which is white,
And others believe it is morn when it's night.

He has tampered with kings, and connived with the Czar;
His Bulgarian twaddle once caused a great war,
Where thousands were slain, but what did he heed,
He still went to Church the lessons to read.

A bumbailey army to Egypt he sent,
In search of some money which long had been spent;
He blew up the forts, then commended his men,
And ordered them back to old England again.

In the far distant Soudan the Mahdi arose,
No doubt he intended to crush all his foes;
But Gladstone sent Gordon, who ne'er was afraid,
Then left him to perish without any aid.

"If I," said poor Gordon, "get out of this place,
That traitor called Gladstone shall ne'er see my face—
To the Congo I'll go, if I am not slain,
And never put foot in old England again."

When the sad news arrived of the fall of Khartoum,
And of how our brave Gordon had met his sad doom,
Gladstone went to the theatre and grinned in a box,
Tho' he knew that old England was then on the rocks.

He allowed the Dutch Boers on Majuba Hill,
Our brave little army to torture and kill ;
And while our poor fellows did welter in gore,
He gave up the sword to the treacherous Boer.

Brave, though black Cetewayo, the great Zulu King,
To civilised England they captive did bring ;
He sent back the Zulu, where first he drew breath,
Unguarded and helpless, to meet his own death.

" Had I done," says Bismark, " so much in my life,
As Gladstone has done in fomenting sad strife,
I could not at this day have looked in the face
Of king, prince or peasant of my noble race."

He has tampered and tarnished his national fame ;
He has injured Great Britain in interest and aim—
Caused strife, war and bloodshed too reckless I ween,
Not caring for honour of England or Queen.

He invokes the great gods their rich blessing to shower,
As he stumps our great nation to get into power ;
E'en now from old Ireland he cravenly begs,
That she will assist him to get on his legs.

Ode to Bacchus.

———⟡———

PURPLE god of joyous wit,
          Here's to thee!
Deign to let the bardic sit
          Near thy knee;
Thy open brow, and laughing eye,
Vanquishing the hidden sigh,
Making care before thee fly,
          Smiling Bacchus, god of wine!

Thy stream intoxicates my song,
          For I am warm;
I love thee late, I love thee long;
          Thou dost me charm;
I ever loved thee much before,
And now I love thee more and more,
For thou art loved the wide world o'er,
          Charming Bacchus, god of wine!

"Angels hear that angels sing,"
          Sang the bard,
While the muse is on the wing,
          Pay regard;
See how Bacchus' nectar flows,
Healing up the heartstrings' woes,
Making friends, and *minus* foes,
          Gracious Bacchus, god of wine!

Ever on thee I depend,
    As my guest ;
Thou wilt bring to me the friend
    I love best ;
Friendship is the wine of love ;
Angels dwell with it above,
Cooing like the turtle-dove
   Lovely Bacchus, god of wine !

Laughing Genius, a " Good night ! "
    Yet, stay awhile !
Ere thou tak'st thy upward flight,
    Upon me smile ;
Drop one feather from thy breast
On the bard, that he may rest,
Then he will be doubly bless'd,
   Glorious Bacchus, god of wine !

Kings are great, but thou art just,
    Night and day ;
What are kings but royal dust—
    Birds of prey ?
Though in splendour they may be—
Menials bow, and bend the knee—
Oh, let me dwell along with thee,
   Famous Bacchus, god of wine !

Sall o' t' Bog.

M I love is like the passion dock,
    That grows i' t'summer fog ;
An' tho' shoo's but a country lass,
    I like mi Sall o' t'Bog.

I walk'd her aght up Rivock End,
    An' dahn a bonny dell,
Whear golden balls an' kahslips grow,
    An' buttercups do smell.

We sat us dahn on top o' t'grass,
    Clois to a runnin' brook,
An' harken'd t'watter wagtails sing
    Wi' t'sparrow, thrush, an' rook.

Aw lockt her in mi arms, an' thowt
    As t'sun shane in her een,
Sho wor the nicest cauliflaar
    At ivver aw hed seen.

'Twor here we tell'd wur tales o' love,
    Beneath t'owd hezzel tree ;
How fondly aw liked Sall o' t'Bog,
    How dearly shoo loved me !

An' if ivver aw deceive thee, Sall,
    Aw vah bi all aw see,
Aw wish 'at aw mud be a kah,
    An' it belong ta thee.

But aw hev plump fergetten nah
    What awther on us said ;
At onny rate we parted friends,
    An' boath went hooam to bed.

Song of the Months.

HIGH o'er the hill-tops moan the wild breezes,
  As from the dark branches I hear the sad strain :
See the lean pauper by his grim hearth he freezes,
  While comfort and plenty in palaces reign.

Dark is the visage of the rugged old ocean,
  To the caves in the billow he rides his foamed steed :
As o'er the grim surge with his chariot in motion,
  He spreads desolation, and laughs at the deed.

No more with the tempest the river is swelling,
  No angry clouds frown, nor sky darkly lower ;
The bee sounds her horn, and the gay news is telling
  That spring is established with sunshine and shower.

In the pride of its beauty the young year is shining,
  And nature with blossom is wreathing the trees ;
The white and the green in rich clusters entwining,
  And sprinkling their sweets on the wings of the
    breeze.

O May, lovely goddess ! what name can be grander ?
  What sunbeam so bright as thine own smiling eye ;
With thy mantle of green, richly spangled in splendour,
  At whose sight the last demon of winter doth fly ?

From her home in the grass see the primrose is peeping,
  While diamond dew-drops around her are spread ;
She smiles thro' her tears like an infant that's sleeping,
  And to laughter is changed as her sorrows are fled.

The landscape around is now sprinkled with flowers,
  The mountains are blue in their distant array ;
The wreaths of green leaves are refreshed with the
    showers,
  Like a moth in the sunshine the lark flies away.

How joyous the reapers their harvest songs singing
  As they see the maid bring the flagon and horn ;
And the goddess of plenty benedictions is flinging
  Over meadows and pastures and barley and corn.

'Tis sweet on the hills with the morning sun shining,
  To watch the rich vale as it brightens below ;
'Tis sweet in the valley when day is declining,
  To mark the fair mountains, deep tinged with its glow.

Now is the time when biting old Boreas,
  True to his calling, the tempests impend ;
His hailstones in fury are pelting before us,
  Our fingers are smarting, and heads they are bent.

The cold winds do murmur, the bleak snow is falling,
  The beasts of the forest from hunger do call ;
There are desolate evenings, comfortless mornings,
  And gloomy noontides for one and for all.

Drear is thine aspect, tyrannical December,
  O hast thou no mercy for the pitiless poor ;
Christmas is thine, and well we remember,
  Though dark is thy visage, we honour thee more.

Bonnie Cliffe Castle.

OH, bonnie Cliffe Castle! what sight can be grander?
    Thou picture of beauty and joy to the eye,
So noble and grand in thy beauty and splendour
    That envy must tremble as she passeth by.

And long may'st thou flourish and bloom like the heather,
    An honour to him who's thy founder so great,
And stand like an oak in both fair and foul weather,
    Till old Father Time hath forgotten thy date.

'Tis a pleasure to view thee from hill-top or level,
    From moorland, from meadow, or mountain afar,
Where Roman pack-horsemen more safely could travel,
    In days when the Briton and Roman waged war.

In those days of yore, from Hawkcliffe to Rivoe,
    The wolf and the wild boar sought after their prey,
But Briton's brave sons amongst them made havoc,
    And thus for Cliffe Castle they opened the way.

Where erst were wild woods, crags, moorlands, and marshes,
    In days long gone by and whose dates are unknown,
Is now the highway where stand thy proud arches,
    Oh, bonnie Cliffe Castle! thou pride of the town.

'Tis true that thy walls were not built for defence,
    Nor that thy equipments befit thee for war;
A castle of love is thy only pretence,
    A name that is higher and nobler by far.

Thou 'mind'st me of five as kind-hearted brothers,
    As ever set sail on the deep ocean's breast,
Whose lives have been spent in love toward others,
    And while blessing others themselves have been blest.

Like heroes of old, on horse or on vessel,
    On land or on water they fought and they won,
And now thy grand towers, O bonnie Cliffe Castle!
    Tower up to the heavens, which answer, "Well done!"

Opening of Devonshire Park,

SEPTEMBER 4TH. 1888.

OH, well do we remember—
    For the news it was so pleasant—
When His Grace the Duke of Devonshire
    Made our famous town a present
Of a pretty little garden—
    An Arcadia in its way—
And how the bells rang merrily
    On that eventful day.

Oh, this lovely little garden
    'Twill be to us a pleasure,
It will delight the great elite—
    To them 'twill be a treasure,
And who are they who dare to say
    The town it did not need one—
A pretty little lovely spot
    And a happy little Eden.

In this pretty little Paradise
   Of beauty and of splendour—
Search our land from end to end,
   You could not find a grander ;
The turtledove can make its love,
   Not caring for the pigeon,
If he belongs his politics
   And follows his religion.

In this pretty little garden,
   When the bloom is on the heather,
Two minds with but one single thought
   Can tell their tales together ;
The maiden from the mansion,
   And the lady from the villa,
Can wander there and shed a tear
   Beneath the weeping willow.

This bonny little garden
   Is fine for perambulators,
Where our handsome servant-lasses
   Can wheel our lovely creatures,
And oh ! how happy they will be !
   As time they are beguiling,
When the mammy and the daddy
   Are upon the babies smiling.

Oh ! this pretty little garden,
   Which every one admires,
Which pleased His Grace the Noble Duke
   To give our little squires.

The news was something wonderful,
   Like the shooting of a rocket,
When they heard that they had got a Park,
   And were "nothing out o'pocket."

In this pretty little garden,
   With all its blossom blooming
We can sit and sing the whole day long,
   From the morning till the gloaming;
And tell Dame Keighley's blunders,
   When her sons were naught but asses;
And could not even raise a Park,
   To please the upper classes.

Then let us give the Noble Duke,
   The praises of the Borough—
For if we did not thank His Grace,
   We should commit an error—
And not forgetting Mr. Leach,
   For he deserves rewarding,
For it is known he got the town
   This pretty little garden.

Farewell to the

REV. H. J. LONGSDON,

Formerly Rector of Keighley.

FAREWELL dear friend, nor take it hard,
    To leave the town where thou hast been,
Where many a joy we hope thou'st had,
    Though witness'd many a sorry scene.

Thy works were good, we know it well,
    We watched thee in thy weary toil;
Where oft obstruction, shame to tell,
    Waits on the good their plans to spoil.

Yet thou dids't toil without a fear
    From day to day, from year to year;
Beloved by all, thy foes are few,
    And they are loth to bid adieu.

We saw thee in the early dawn
    Up with the lark at break of morn,
Thy duties promptly to attend,
    Our shepherd, pastor, and our friend.

With good advice to one and all,
    The old, the young, the great, the small;
In lane or house, in church or street,
    Thy presence we were glad to meet.

" Thou art a man ! a man ! a man ! "
  The Poet quotes from some old play ;
" An upright, honest gentleman,
  Whose likes we meet not every day."

And when thou leavest us behind,
  Our recollections will not die—
Of thee whose meekness, zeal, and love,
  Are known alike to low and high.

Out from thy fold, all other flocks
  Were proud of thee—a shepherd true,
All other shepherds greeted thee,
  Although thy flocks to theirs were few.

Thou tended with a shepherd's care,
  And saw that none did go astray ;
Thou led them with an honest will,
  From early morn to evening's ray.

Adieu, dear sir, long may'st thou live
  To be a credit to our isle ;
And when thou toil'st 'midst other friends,
  May fortune on thy labours smile.

He's Thy Brother.

TURN from the rich thy steps awhile,
  And visit this poor domicile ;
Abode of flavours rank and vile?
This is the home, and this the style,
              Where lives thy brother !

The cobwebs are his chandeliers ;
Bricks and dank straw his bed and chairs ;
He has no carpet on the stairs,
But, like the wild beasts to their lairs,
              Crawls in thy brother.

He once did stride his father's knee —
A little horseman bold and free ;
And, should thou trace this pedigree,
Thy mother's darling pet was he—
              Thy little brother.

His mind was not of thine, 'tis plain ;
He dreamt of wonders, thou of gain ;
But thou thy object didst attain
For which another sought in vain—
              E'en thy own brother.

Thou cunningly didst keep thy pace,
While he joined in the wild-goose chase ;
Thou'rt now the great one of this place,
While he hath lost his phantom race—
              Thy wretched brother !

I see a form amongst the crowd,
With stricken heart, and head that's bowed;
I hear a voice, both deep and loud—
A voice of one that wanted food—
    It is thy brother.

The meanest wretch that ever trod,
The smallest insect 'neath the sod,
Are creatures of an All-seeing God,
Who may have smitten with his rod
    Thy foolish brother.

He careth not for wealth or show,
But dares thee to neglect, e'en now,
That unmanned wretch, so poor and low,
Else he may deal a heavy blow,
    E'en for thy brother.

Lund's Excursion to Windermere.

COME hither mi muse, an' li!t me a spring,
 Tho' daghtless awhile tha's been on the wing;
But yet tha mun try to cum up ta t'mark,
An' give us sum rhyme for a bit of a lark:
An' tho' at thy notes in this sensation age,
Wiseacres may giggle an' critics may rage,
Thou art my sole hobby there is no mistake,
So sing us t'Excursion ta Windermere Lake.

'Twor a fine summer's mornin' as ivver wor seen,
All nature wor wearin' her mantle o' green ;
The birds wor all singin' i' owd Cockle Wood,
As if by their notes they all understood,
As weel as the people who com wi' a smile,
To see the procession march off i' grand style.

" Owd Rowland," the bell wi' his gert iron tongue,
Proclaim'd to the people both owd an' young,
'Twor high time to rise for each moment wor dear
As t'train wod be startin' fer Lake Windermere ;
An' Rowland, the bell, didn't toll, sir, i' vain,
For hunderds wur ready ta start for the train.

But harken what music—grand music is here,
Ower maantains, dahn valleys, it's saanding so clear ;
It's t'Turkey Mill Band wi ther sharps and ther flats,
I' ther blue an' green coits an' ther red-toppin'd hats,
'Tis plain whear they're bahn wi' t'long paces they take,
An' they'll play wi' some vengeance at Windermere Lake

But, harken ageean ! what's comin' this way ?
More music, grand music ; hey, hear how they play !
It's t'Fife an' Drum Band fra Throttlepoke Raw,
Wi' as strong a big drummer as ivver yah saw,
An' both his drum ends must be solid as stone,
Fer bi t'way 'at he thumps he macks it fair groan.

The procession moves off in a double quick pace,
An' all seem delightful - a smile on ther face,
As the music strikes up wi' owd " Robin a Dair,"
Toan hauf o' t'wimmen scarce knaw what they ail ;
To see the bands marching it wod yah delight,
So ably conducted by owd Jimmy Wright.

The weivers led on by Miss Hob an' Miss Hall,
Each dress'd i' ther jackets, new turban, an' fall,
An' if you'd o' seen 'em you'd o' thowt they wor fine,
Wi' ther nice parasols an' ther gert crinoline ;
But as they wor marchin' foaks sed at Miss Hob,
Wor t'nicest and smartest young woman i' t'job,

T'next section 'at followed wor a section o' rakes,
Led on by owd blossom, an' Driver o' Jacques,
Wi' Ruddock an' Rufus, an' Snowball so breet;
Along wi' owd Nathan, Bill Rollin an' Wreet ;
An' Harry O'Bridget, Tom Twist, an' his pals,
An' Benger, an' Capper, an' Jonas o Salls.

The lads an' the lasses come marchin' behind,
An' rare an' weel suited wor t'youngsters yo mind ;
For all wor nah waitin' fer t'Fife an' Drum Band,
To strike up like thunner ther music so grand ;
How prahd an' delighted yo might a seen some,
When t'drummer wi' vengeance wor thumpin' his drum.

An' who cud hev thowt it ?—but let ma go on ;—
There wor Jacky o' Squires an' Cowin' Heead John,
Wi' Corney o' Rushers, but not bi hissen,
For there wor Joseph o' Raygills, owd Jess an' owd Ben.
Ye sall seek fer a month, but between nah an' then,
I defy ye ta find sitch a pick'd lot o' men.

Tom Nicholl then marched at t'heead of his clan,
An' it's said 'at he muster'd his men to a man ;
There wor Joaney o' Bobs, an' his mates full o' glee,
An' that little dark fella 'at comes fra t'Gooise Ee.
All a set o' fine fellas in heighest respect,
Weel up i' moustaches an' nicely shirt-neckt.

But among the procession at walk'd in his pride,
Wor Joey o' Willie's 'at lives at t'Beck Side ;
An' along wi' Bill Earby wor marchin' his friend,
Wun Jemmy o' Roses fra t'Branshaw Moor End.
As we pass'd dahn t'tahn the foaks did declare
'At t'best lukin' men wor Sam Butt an' Black Hare.

But t'next at com on an' made t'biggest crack,
Wor t'gallant Big-benners led on wi' Bill Shack ;
An' t'spectators praised 'em an' seem'd i' ther joy,
When they saw Johnny Throstle, an' Nolan an' Boy.
Altho' not weel up i' ther armour an mail,
Yet these are the lads 'at can tell yu a tale.

Habsumivver, we push'd an' thrusted thro' t'craad,
Wal we landed at t station an' waited i' t'yard ;
So we all sattled dahn, for we thowt it t'best plan
To wait o' wer orders to get into t'train.

Habsumivver, after a deal o' yellin' an' screamin' o'
t'injuns, Mr. Mann sed all wor reight nah, an' they
mud start as sooin as they liked, for ivverybody wor i'
t'train at wor bahn, but owd Pally Pickles an' Matty o'
Maude's ; an' their Sally cudn't go becos they had a
mustard plaister to put on to their Roger's chest ; he'd
strain'd his lungs wi' eitin' cahcumbers. Beside, owd
Pally cudn't go either, becos shoo'd nobody to wait on
t'owd fella at wor laid up i' t'merly grubs ; an' ivverybody wor so taen on abaght Will Scott not going, for,
as owd Betty sed, what wod they do if ther legs gat
asleep an' no galvanic battery to shack em reight
ageean ?

But, hahsumivver, t'guard blew his whistle an' off
t'train started helter-skelter up bi Utley as hard as
ivver it cud go. An nah for a change o' scene!—fer
t'Exley-Heeaders aght wi ther rhubub pasties an' treacle
parkins. Harry o' Bridget's hed a treacle parkin t'size
of a pancake in his hat crahn, an' Joe o' owd Grace's fra
Fell Loin hed a gert bacon collop in his pocket t'size of
a oven tin. Somebody remarks, " Tha'll grease thi
owd chops wi' that, Joe." He sed " I like a bit o' bacon
when it isn't reezed, tha knaws, especially home-fed
like this "; but just when he wor exhibitin' it rhaand
t'hoile, t'train stopp'd at Kilwick Station, fer t'maister
an' t'missis wor waitin' to get in; so t'Turkey Mill Band
struck up " We're goin' home to glory," wi' credit to
both t'conductors an' thersens. Hahsumivver, they
wor forced to put double time in at t'latter end, for
Puffin' Billy started o' screaming ageean fearfully, so
all wor in t'carriages an' off in a crack—my word, they
did leg it ower hedges an' dykes, thru valleys an'
mahntains—

> " Where the wind nivver blew,
>
> Nor a cock ivver crew,
>
> Nor the deil sahnded
>
> His Bugle Horn."

I'll assure yu, foak, it seemed varry little afoar
we wor at Clapham. Why, yu can judge for yersens;
when Tom o' Twist's gat up an' popped his heead aght
o' t'window an' shaated aaght " We're at Derby
already!" but it turned aght to be nowt but a coil
truck wi' " Derby " marked on it. Well, be it as it may,

we landed at Lancaster sooin, an' some o' t'owd maids
gat aght here, but it wor nivver knawn to this day
what for; hahsumivver, it hes been suspected at they
wor after some watter, for ther shooin wor steepin' wet
when they com back. But yu mun knaw at after a
deal o' twistin' an' twinin' they started for Windermere,
but, my word, it worrant generally thowt so, for owd
Nathan o' Johnny's an' their Samuel, an' owd Matty o'
Sykes's, an' Bob o' t'Bog, stood it boldly 'at it wor
goin' back to Keighley, an' wodant believe it wal they
reitched Kendal; besides, ivverybody thowt at t'train
wor lost, but after another start we landed at
Windermere, an' nearly all t'passengers wor fair
capp'd, for they thowt for sewer at t'injun hed been flaid
wi' summat.

> But, hod yer din, says Railway Tim,
>   As it is varry clear,
> At t'injun's reight an' landed streight,
>   For this is Windermere.

So, i' landing, ivverbody seemed quite startled wi'
t'appearance o' t'place. "Well, if ivver, I'm fair
capp'd!", sed owd Maude o' Peter's, "it's t'nicest spot
I ivver saw wi' mi een, an' I sall say so to mi deein'
day. It looks like a paradise! I've seen mony a nice
place i' mi life-time, both dreamin' an' wakin', but
this licks all! What wi' t'grand black marble houses
an' t'roses growin' up at t'front, it's ommost like bein'
i' Heaven." But nobody cud hear aboon t'toan hauf
o' what wor said cos t'bands wor playin' as hard as
ivver they cud an' t'foak wor all in a bussle, for—

Miss Hob an' Miss Jonas tuke a cab dahn to Bowness,
    An' mind yu, they luk'd fearful grand ;
An' when they gat theer they tuke fer Grassmere,
    Like two o' t'first ladies i' t'land.

Miss Walsh an' Miss Roddy an' another young body,
    Bethowt 'em 'at it wod be t'best,
To tak a fine boat an' just hev a float
    Dahn the lake as far as Dove's Nest.

Says Miss Nelly Holmes, "as I've left off mi looms
    I'll show at I'm summat better ;
An' I'll go ta Low Wood, it might do ma good,
    An' sport both on t'land an' on t'watter."

Hahsumivver, Miss Martha Smith fra Utley, an
owd maid, an' Jenny Hodgson, an' Ann Shack, an'
abaght nineteen other owd maids, bethowt 'em they'd
hev some teah, for there wor a paper stuck i' ivvery
window wi' "Hot water sold here," as an inscription.
So they went in an' bargain'd for it, an' ax'd what it
wor a piece fer hot watter. "Tuppence a piece," says
t'Missis. "Tuppence a piece!" exclaim'd t'dollop of
'em, "we can get it at owd Matty Wreet's fer a penny
a week. It's a burning shame, but let's hev a bucket
a piece."

    So thirteen cups a piece they tuke,
        An' they were noan ta blame,
    Fer weel shoo knew did Hannah Shack,
        They'd hev to pay the same.

An' my word, t'gert foak wor capp'd when they saw
us ; there wor some squintin' throo glasses, yu mind,

an' especially when t'band started a playin'. In fact,
they wor fair charm'd wi' t'Turkey Mill Banders, an' a
deal o' t'young ladies an' gentlemen admired t'conductor, fer his arm went just like a hand-loom weiver
swingin' his pickin' stick.

> Fer monny a noble lord did say,
>   An' so did monny a heiress,
> "Can this be Julien's Band, I pray,
>   That late we've seen in Paris.
>
> "Upon my word, I think it is
>   That famous French instructor,
> Mon Dieu! when I behold his phiz,
>   It is the great conductor."

But they wor t'moast capped wi' t'Fife an' Drum
Band ov owt. They tuke 'em to be a band of
Esquimaux at hed just lan'ed i' England. Hahsumivver, we followed after, marchin' ta t'tune 'at t'owd
kah deed on, i' droves like a squad o' pie-bald geese,
wal we com ta t'watter edge, an' then—

> To Miller's Brah, an' Calf-garth Woods,
>   Some on 'em tuke ther route,
> Some sailed across to Castle Wray,
>   An' some went whear they thowt.
>
> Some tuke a yacht to Newby Brig,
>   To brave both wind an' tide,
> Wal others sailed around Belle Isle,
>   An' some to Ambleside.

I' landin' at Ambleside, Joe o' Raygill's bethowt him
he'd hev a glass o' ale, an' bethegs he'd t'misfortun

to leave three gert curnberry pasties i' t'hotel, an'
didn't bethink him wal he'd getten on ta t'top of a big
hill, but when he bethowt him, my word, he did bounce
dahn that hill ta some tune. When he gat back,
t'missis hed geen 'em to Jonas o' Sall's, an' behold
they wor luking fer one another up hills an' dahn
valleys, Joe axin' ivverybody he met if they'd seen
owt of his three pasties, an' Jonas axin' fer t'owner on
'em. Hahsumivver, they nivver gat ta see nowt wal
they wor theer, for they didn't meet wal t'train wor
just startin' back agean, an' then Joe didn't get his
pasties, cos Jonas hed geen 'em to a injun-driver, an'
theer—betmess he'd hetten 'em, ta Joe's mortification
an' rage !

But, that worn't all t'mistak at wor made ; fer Bill
Rollins bethowt him at he'd lost summat, but cudn't
tell fer his life what it wor. He groped his pockets,
luk'd into his carpet beg, an' studied fer aboon an haar ;
at last he pick'd it aght 'at it wor their Peg 'at he'd
lost somewheer up on t'mahntens.

Well, as I wor tellin' yu, we'd promenaded t'
gigantic hills an' beantiful valleys, intermix'd wi'
ower-hingin' peaks an' romantic watter-falls which form
part o' t'grand Lake scenery of ahr English Switzerland to the delight of ivvery one o' t'excursionists.
T'day beginnin' to advance, an' "back agean"
bein' t'word i' ivverybody's maath, yu cud see t'fowk
skippin' ower t'Lake ("Home-ward bound," as t'song
says), some in a Indian canoe, some in a Venetian
gondolier ; owd Ben Rusher wor in a Chinese junk,
somebody sed. But, haivver, hunderds mud be seen
on board o' t'steam yachts comin' fra Newby Brig an'
Ambleside. Fra t'latter place t'steamer wor fair

craaded wi' foak, for i' t'first class end ther wor Mr.
an' Mrs. Lund an' their illustrious friends, Mr. Mann
an' staff wi' a parson an' four of his handsome
dowters; at t'other end wor a German Band, some
niggers, Jimmy Wright, jun., alias Jim o' Peggy's, wi'
a matter o' one hunderd Ranters rhaand him. Jim
wod hev his lip in; but he's a rare chorus singer,
there's nowt abaght that; for, my word, t'strangers
did praise him aboon a bit, an' weel he desarved it, fer
he gap'd like a young throstle, wal t'foak wor fair
charm'd, an' 'specially t'Germans an' t'niggers 'at wor
on deck, fer they'd nivver heeard onny chorus-singin'
afoar they heeard Jim strike up—

<blockquote>
We're joyously sailin' ower the lake,
  Bound fer t'opposite shore;
An' which o' yu's fooil enuff ta believe
  We sall nivver see land onny more.

  Let the hurrican roar,
  Sall we ivver land onny more.

The skilful pilot's at the wheel,
  An' his mate is watchin' near;
So the captain shouts " Cheer up, mi lads,
  There's nobody nowt to fear."

  Then let the hurrican roar,
  We sall reitch the opposite shore.
</blockquote>

An' summat abaght " the evergreen shore " he sang.
But what wi' t'beautiful landscapes on both sides o'
t'Lake, an' t'recollections o' Wordsworth, Wilson,
Mrs. Hemans, Harriet Martineau, an' other famous
poets, painters, an' authors, it threw one of our party
into a kind o' poetical mood—

For wal he stood upon the deck,
　　He oft wor heeard to say,
" I'd raither come to Windermere,
　　Nor go to Morecambe Bay ;
An' though I've been to Malsis Hall,
　　Where it is fearful grand,
It's nowt at all compared wi' this—
　　The nicest place i' t'land.

For, O how splendid is the Lake,
　　Wi' scenery like this !
If I end nobbut stop a week,
　　It wod be nowt amiss ;
A resolution nah I'll maak,
　　T'next summer what to do ;—
Astecad o' comin' for a day,
　　I'll stop a week or two."

But nah we land at Bowness Pier,
　　Then sooin we jump ashore,
An' back to t'Station we did steer,
　　For rare an' pleased we wor :
So into t'train for back agean,
　　Owd friends once more to meet ;
An' in a crack we're landed back—
　　Bi ten o'clock at neet.

All join i' praise to Mr. Mann,
　　For t'management he made ;
An' praise the gallant Turkey Band,
　　For t'music 'at they play'd :
An' praise is due fra ivvery one
　　'At shared i' this diversion ;
All praise an' thanks to Mr. Lund,
　　Who gav this grand Excursion.

The Tartan Plaid.

IN Auld Lang Syne I've heard 'em say
   My granny then she wore
A bonnie Scottish Tartan Plaid
   In them good days o' yore ;
An' weel I ken when I was young
   Some happy days we had,
When ladies they were dress'd so gay
   In Scottish Tartan Plaid.

Me thinks I see my father now
   Sat working at his loom—
I see my mother at the wheel—
   In our dear village home ;
The swinging-stick I hear again,
   Its buzzin' makes me sad,
To think those happy days are gone
   When weaving Tartan Plaid.

It is not in a clannish view,
   For clans are naught to me,
But 'tis our ancient Tartan Plaid
   I dearly love to see.
'Tis something grand ye will agree
   To see a Highland lad,
Donn'd in his celtic native garb,
   The grand old Tartan Plaid.

Our Soldier lads in tartan kilts
   Outshine our warriors bold
(Who dress in scarlet, green, and blue,
   Decked off with shining gold) ;
Just see our kilted lads so brave,
   It makes my heart feel glad,
And 'minds me of my boyish days
   When dress'd in Tartan Plaid.

"O wad some power" the hint we give
   Our Sovereign Lady Queen,
To dress herself and lady maids
   In bonnie tartan sheen.
Then treadles, shuttles, warp, and weft—
   (For trade would not be bad)—
Would rattle as in days of yore,
   When weaving Tartan Plaid.

The Pauper's Box.

THOU odious box, as I look on thee,
   I wonder wilt thou be unlocked for me ?
No, no ! forbear !—yet then, yet then,
'Neath thy grim lid do lie the men—
Men whom fortune's blasted arrows hit,
And send them to the pauper's pit.

O dig a grave somewhere for me,
Deep underneath some wither'd tree ;
Or bury me on the wildest heath,
Where Boreas blows his wildest breath,
Or 'mid some wild romantic rocks :
But, oh ! forbear the pauper's box.

Throw me into the ocean deep,
Where many poor forgotten sleep ;
Or fling my corpse in the battle mound,
With coffinless thousands 'neath the ground ;
I envy not the mightiest dome,
But save me from a pauper's tomb.

I care not if t'were the wild wolf's glen,
Or the prison yard, with wicked men :
Or into some filthy dung-hole hurled—
Anywhere, anywhere ! out of the world !
In fire or smoke on land or sea,
Than thy grim lid be closed on me.

But let me pause, ere I say more
About thee, unoffending door ;
When I bethink me, now I pause,
It is not thee who makes the laws,
But villians who, if all were just,
In thy grim cell would lay their dust.

But yet, t'were grand beneath yond wall,
To lie with friends,—relations all ;
If sculptured tombstones were not there,
But simple grass with daisies fair ;
And were it not, grim box, for thee
'Twere paradise, O cemetery.

The Vale of Aire.

[It was early in the morning that I took my ramble. I had noticed but little until I arrived at the foot of the quaint old hamlet of Marley. My spirits began to be cheered, for lively gratitude glowed in my heart at the wild romantic scenery before me. Passing the old mansion, I wended my way towards the huge crag called the " Altar Rock." Wild and rugged as the scenery was, it furnished an agreeable entertainment to my mind, and with pleasure I pushed my way to the top of the gigantic rock, where I viewed the grandeur of the vale below. The blossom on the branches, the crooked Aire gliding along like sheets of polished crystal, made me poetic. I thought of Nicholson, the poet of this beautiful vale, and reclining on a green moss-covered bank, I framed these words.]

POET Nicholson, old Ebor's darling bard,
    Accept from me at least one tributary line ;
Yet how much more should be thy just reward,
    Than any wild unpolished song of mine.

No monument in marble can I raise,
    Or sculptured bust in honour of thy name ;
Let humbly try to celebrate thy praise,
    And give applause that thou shouldst duly claim.

All hail, the songsters that awake the morn,
 And soothe the soul with wild melodious strains :
All hail, the rocks that Bingley hills adorn,
 Beneath whose shades wild Nature's grandeur reigns.

From off yon rock that rears its head so high,
 And overlooks the crooked river Aire ;
While musing Nature's works full meet the eye,
 The envied game, the lark and timid hare.

In Goitstock Falls, and rugged Marley's hill,
 In Bingley's grand and quiet sequestered dale,
Each silvery stream, each dike or rippled rill,
 I see thy haunt and read thy " Poacher's Tale."

So, Homer-like, thy harp was wont to tune
 Thy native vale in glorious days of old,
Whose maidens fair in virtuous beauty shone—
 Her sages and her heroes great and bold.

No flattering baseness could employ thy mind,
 The free-born muse detests that servile part :
In simple lore thy self-taught lay I find
 More grandeur far than all the gloss of art.

Though small regard be paid to worth so rare,
 And humble worth unheeded pass along ;
Ages to come will sing the " Vale of Aire,"
 Her Nicholson and his historic song.

Fra Haworth ta Bradford.

FRA Haworth tahn the other day,
   Bi t'route o' Thornton Height,
Joe Hobble an' his better hauf,
   Went inta Bradford straight.

Nah Joe ta Bradford hed been before,
   But shoo hed nivver been ;
But hahsumivver they arrived
   Safe inta t'Bowlin' Green.

They gav a lad a parkin pig,
   As on the street they went ;
Ta point 'em aght St. George's Hall,
   An' Ostler's Monument.

Bud t'little jackanapes bein' deep,
   An' thowt they'd nivver knaw,
Show'd Joseph Hobble an' his wife
   T'first monument he saw.

As sooin as Joe gat up ta t'rails,
   His een blaz'd in his heead ;
Exclamin', they mud just as weel
   A gooan an' robb'd the deead.

Bud whoivver's ta'en them childer dahn,
   Away fra poor owd Dick,
Desarves his heead weel larapin,
   Wi' a dahn gooid hazel stick.

T'lad seein' Joe froth aght o' t'maath,
   He sooin tuke to his heels,
For astead o' t'Ostler's Monument,
   He'd shown 'em Bobby Peel's.

The Veteran.

I LEFT yon fields so fair to view ;
    I left yon mountain pass and peaks ;
I left two een so bonny blue,
    A dimpled chin and rosy cheeks.
For an helmet gay and suit o' red
    I did exchange my corduroy ;
I mind the words the Sergeant said,
    When I in sooth was but a boy.

"Come, rouse my lad, be not afraid ;
    Come, join and be a brave dragoon :
You'll be well clothed, well kept, well paid,
    To captain be promoted soon.
Your sweetheart, too, will smile to see
    Your manly form and dress so fine ;
Give me your hand and follow me,—
    Our troop's the finest in the line.

" The pyramids beheld our corps
    Drive back the mighty man of Fate !
Our ire is felt on every shore,
    In every country, clime, or state.
The Cuirassiers at Waterloo
    We crushed ;—they were the pride of France !
At Inkerman, with sabre true,
    We broke the Russ and Cossack lance !

" Then come, my lad, extend your hand,
    Tame indolence I hold it mean ;
Now follow me, at the command,
    Of our Most Gracious Sovereign Queen !

A prancing steed you'll have to ride ;
  A bonny plume will deck your brow ;
With clinking spurs and sword beside,—
  Come! here's the shilling : take it now!"

The loyal pledge I took and gave,—
  It was not for the silver coin ;
I wished to cross the briny wave,
  And England's gallant sons to join.
Since—many a summer's sun has set,
  An' time's graved-care is on my brow,
Yet I am free and willing yet
  To meet old England's daring foe.

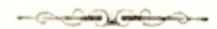

Address to the Queen,

JUNE 20th, 1887.

To the Queen's Most Excellent Majesty.

MOST Gracious Sovereign Lady, Victoria Alexandra Guelph, Queen of the hearts of her people throughout all civilisation, one of your Majesty's loyal and faithful subjects desires most respectfully to approach your Majesty to congratulate you upon the completion of the fiftieth year of your reign. In the same year of your Majesty's coronation, in a wild part of old Yorkshire, where it is said the wind never blew nor the cock ever crew, was your Most Gracious Majesty's humble servant born ; and at the very hour that your Majesty ascended the Throne,

a kind, good Yorkshire mother was rocking her baby
in an old oak cradle, while the father was treading the
treadles and picking the shuttle of his old hand-loom
to the tune of "Britons never shall be slaves"; and I
am proud to convey to your Majesty that the child in
the old oak cradle was no less a person than your
Majesty's humble and obedient servant, Bill o'th'
Hoylus End, Poet and Philosopher to the plebians of
Keighley, and who now rejoices in the fiftieth year of
your Majesty's reign that he has been blessed with
good health during that long period, having had at no
time occasion to call in a physician. John Barleycorn
has been my medical adviser, and when I begin to
review the fifty years of your most illustrious reign,
from my birth, I feel grateful indeed, for great and
mighty men and nations have risen and fallen; but I
am proud to think that your Most Gracious Majesty
and your humble servant have weathered the storm,
and I also can assure your Majesty that the lukewarm
loyalty of the upper ten is not a sample of people here,
for during the latter half of your Majesty's reign up
to now prosperity has shone upon the once crooked,
old, mis-shapen town, for wealth has been accumulated
to the tune of millions, which I am sorry to inform
your Majesty is in the hands of those who mean to
keep it. One portion of your Majesty's lukewarm
loyal subjects have the advancement of art and science
so much on the brain that it is feared they will go
stark mad. I have also much pleasure in informing
your gracious Majesty that His Grace the Duke of
Devonshire has presented the people of Keighley with
a plot of ground to be called the Devonshire Park,
which will be opened on the occasion of your Majesty's
Jubilee; also that Henry Isaac Butterfield, Esquire,

of bonny Cliffe Castle, has erected a noble-looking
structure, to be called the Jubilee Tower, which will
be opened on the day of your Majesty's Grand
Jubilee, to commemorate your Majesty's glorious
reign. This gentleman is a native of Keighley, and
fairly entitled to be knighted by your gracious Majesty,
seeing that he has done more to beautify the town than
all the rest It has also been given out that the town
has to be honoured by a royal visit from your
Majesty's grandson, Prince George. But pray take a
fool's advice, your Majesty, and don't let him come
unless he is able to pay his own expenses; for I can
assure His Royal Highness that this is the city of
number oneism. Yet with the exception of parting
with the bawbees, I dare be sworn that your Majesty's
subjects in Keighley are the grand and genuine men
of the shire, take them in art and science, flood or
field.

I sincerely hope that your Most Gracious Majesty
will excuse the blunt and out-spoken Bard, who will
ever remain your Majesty's most humble and obedient
servant,—BILL O'TH' HOYLUS END.

P.S.—I beg your Majesty's most humble pardon, for
since I addressed your most gracious Majesty a
note has come to me stating that the Brewers,
Bakers, Shoemakers, and Tailors, have subscribed
and bought a splendid Ox, which will be roasted
and served to the poor on the occasion of the
celebration of your most gracious Majesty's Jubilee.

THEN Hail to England's Gracious Queen !
   'Tis now proclaimed afar,
The Jubilee of our Gracious Queen,
   The Empire's Guiding Star.

For fifty years she's been to us
    A Monarch and a Mother;
And looks her subjects in the face
    As Sister or a Brother.

Then here's a health to England's Queen
    Whom Jove to us hath given;
A better Monarch ne'er has been
    Beneath His starry heaven.
There is no man of any clan,
    O'er any land or sea,
But what will sing "God bless our Queen"
    On her grand Jubilee.

The world looks on Old England's Queen
    In danger for protection;
Nor never yet hath England failed
    To make her grand correction.
"Fair play," she cries, no one shall harm
    A child beneath my realm;
I'm Captain of Great Britain's barque
    And standing at the helm.

Had England trusted wicked men,
    This day where had she been?
But lo! she had a Guiding Star,
    'Twas our dear Mother Queen.
There is no foe, where'er you go
    This day, I vow, could hate her;
She's a blessing to her nation,
    And a terror to a traitor.

As she has been, long may she reign,
  The Grand Old Queen of Britain ;
In letters of bright gold her name
  Henceforward should be written.
All nations 'neath the stars above,
  And canopy of heaven,
Rejoice to see her Jubilee
  In Eighteen Eighty-seven.

Ode to Burns on his 130th Birthday.

WEAK bard, but thou dost try in vain
    To tune that mighty harp again,
To try thy muse in Burns's strain—
        Thou'rt far behind.
And yet to praise him thou would'st fain—
        It is thy mind.

He who sang of Bruce's command
At Bannockburn, with sword in hand,
And bid his warriors firmly stand
        Upon the spot ;
And bid the foemen leave the land,
        Or face the Scot.

He who freed the human mind
Of superstitions weak and blind ;
He who peered the scenes behind
        Their holy fairs—
How orthodox its pockets lined
        With canting prayers.

Yes ; he whose life's short span appears
Mixed up with joyous smiles and tears ;
So interwove with doubts and fears
        His harp did ring ;
And made the world to ope' its ears
        And hear him sing.

'Twas his to walk the lonely glen,
Betimes to shun the haunts of men,
Searching for his magic pen —
        Poetic fire :
And far beyond the human ken
        He strung the lyre.

And well old Scotland may be proud
To hear her Burns proclaimed aloud,
For to her sons the world hath bowed
        Through Burns's name—
All races of the world are proud
        Of Burns's fame.

Trip to Malsis Hall.

THE day wor fine, the sun did shine,
   No signs o' rain to fall,
When t'North Beck hands, i' jovial bands,
   Did visit Malsis Hall.

Up by the hill o' North Beck Mill,
   Both owd an' young did meet;
To march I trow, i' two-by-two,
   Procession dahn the street.

An' Marriner's Band, wi' music grand,
   Struck up wi' all ther might;
Then one an' all, both great an' small,
   March'd on wi' great delight.

The girls an' boys, wi' jovial noise,
   The fife an' drum did play;
For ivvery one wod hev some fun
   On this eventful day.

Owd Joan o' Sall's wi' all his pals,
   March'd on wi' all ther ease:
Just for a lark, some did remark,
   " There goes some prime owd cheese!"

T'Exl' Heead chaps wi' their girt caps,
   An' coits nut quite i' t'fashion;
Wi' arms ding-dong, they strut along,
   An' put a famous dash on.

Tom Wilkins dress'd up in his best,
   T'owd wife put on her fall,
Fer they wor bent, what com or went,
   To dine at Malsis Hall.

Ther wor Tommy Twist among the list,
   Wi' his magenta snaht ;
He's often said sin he gat wed,
   T'owd lass sud hev an aght.

Among the lot wor owd Sam Butt,
   As fine as owd Lord Digby ;
An' owd Queer Doos, wi' his streit shoes,
   An' wi' him Joseph Rigby.

There's Jimmy Gill, o' Castle Hill,—
   That gentleman wi' t'stick,—
There's Will an' Sam, an' young John Lamb,
   An' Ben an' Earby Dick.

I scorn to lie—the reason why
   It is a shame awm sure !
But among the job wor owd Joe Hob,
   Behold ! a perfect kewer.

I'd quite forgot, among the lot,
   There too wor Pally Pickles,
Wi' crinoline shoo walks so fine,
   Shoo's like a cat i' prickles.

Bud to mi tale—aw mussant fail
   I' owt on this occasion—
Wi' heead erect, an' girt respect,
   We march to Keighley Station.

Nah—all reight fain gat into t'train,
   Owd Ned began to scream ;
Then Master Pratt doft off his hat,
   An' just pept aght at t'steeam.

This jovial band when they did land,
   Got off the train so hearty,
For they all went, wi' that intent,
   To hev a grand tea-party !

The country foak did gape an' luke,
   To see us all delighted,
An' ivvery one did say " Begum,
   Aw wish awd been invited."

'Tis joy to tell, they marched as well
   As t'Scots did ower the border,
Owd Wellington an' all his men
   Ne'er saw such marchin' order.

The lookers-on, to see them come,
   Gat on ta t'second storey ;
Reight dahn the park they did 'em mark,
   Comin' i' their full glory.

Then to the place each smilin' face,
   Moved on i' grand succession ;
The lookers on did say " Well done,
   It is a grand procession !"

When they'd all pass'd the hall at last
   They form'd into a column ;
Then Jimmy Wreet, wi' all his meet,
   Gav aght a hymn so solemn :

Then all did raise their voice i' praise,
   Wi' music in the centre ;
They sang a hymn i' praise o' Him,
   'At is the girt Creator.

That bit bein' done, they all did run,
   To get a pleasant day in,

Some went there, an' some went here,
    An' t'Bands began o' playin'.

Wi' mich amaze, we all did gaze,
    Arahnd this splendid park ;
Then little Jake began to talk,
    An' thus he did remark : —

" At Morecambe Bay I've been a day,
    At Bolton Woods an' Ilkley ;
But Malsis Hall outstrips 'em all,
    'At I've seen aght o' Keighley."

The girt park wall arahnd the hall,
    Majestical does stand ;
Wi' wavin' trees, an' pleasant breeze,
    It's like a fairy land.

It fill'd wur eyes wi' gert surprise,
    To see the fahnten sporting ;
An' on the top, stuck on a prop,
    The British flags wor floatin'.

The walks so grand, wi' yellow sand,
    An' splendid wor the pavin',
High over all, arahnd the wall,
    Wor flags an' banners wavin'.

Nah—some made fun, an' some did run,
    Owd women they wor singin'—
" Do you ken the Moofin Man,"—
    An' others they wor swingin'.

I' sooth 'twor grand to see this band,
    Assembled all together ;
Bud sad to say, that varry day
    Turn'd aght some shockin' weather.

Bud war ner t'rain, aw mun explain,
   'At caus'd a girt disaster,
All but one sort o' breead ran short—
   It wor no fault o' t'maister.

O, Gormanton! thy breead an' bun,
   An' judgment it wor scanty;
Oh, what a shame, an' what a name,
   For not providing plenty!

Oh, silly clown! thah might hev knawn,
   To eyt each one wor able;
The country air did mak some swear
   They cud onmost eyt a table.

The atmosphere, no longer clear,
   The clouds are black an' stormy;
Then all but one away did run,
   Like some desertin' army.

On—on! they go! as if some foe
   Wor chargin' at the lot!
If they got there, they didn't care
   A fig for poor Will Scott!

Poor lame owd Will remains theer still,
   His crutches hes to fetch him;
But he's seen t'time, when in his prime,
   'At nobody theer cud catch him.

Like some fast steed wi' all its speed,
   All seem'd as they wor flyin';
To escape the rain, an' catch the train,
   Both owd and young wor tryin'.

One Mat o' Wills, abaght Crosshills,
 He heeard a fearful hummin',
He said ta t'wife, " Upon mi life,
 Aw think the French are comin' !

Tha knaws reight weel 'at we've heeard tell
 O' sich strange things afore,
So lass luke quick an' cut thi stick,
 An' I will bolt the door."

Like drahnded rats they pass owd Mat's,
 An' ran dahn to the station ;
Owd Betty Bake an' Sally Shacks
 Were both plump aght o' patience.

" This is a mess," says little Bess,
 'At lives on t'top o' t'garden ;
" There's my new shawl an' fine lace fall,
 They'll nut be worth a fardin."

But, hark ! ding-dong goes through the throng,
 The bell does give the sign,
Wi' all its force, the iron horse
 Comes trottin' dahn the line.

Then one by one they all get in,
 Wet, fatigued, an' weary ;
The steam does blow, owd Ned doth go,
 An' we come back so cherry.

Whene'er we roam away fra hooam,
 No matter wheer or when,
In storm or shower, if in wur power,
 To home, sweet home, we turn !

The Bold Buchaneers:

A Military description of the Second Excursion to
Malsis Hall, the Residence of JAMES LUND, Esq.

———

I REMEMBER perusing when I was a boy,
    The immortal bard Homer—his siege of old Troy,
So the Malsis encampment I'll sing if you will,
How our brave army "bivoked" on the plains o'
    Park Hill.

Near the grand Hall o' Malsis our quarters we took,
When Lieutenant-col. Don Frederick spoke,
Commanding his aid-de-camp Colonel de Mann,
To summons and muster the chiefs o' the clan.

Majors Wood, Lamb, and Pollard came up to the lines,
Each marching their companies up to the nines;
The twirlers and twisters, the knights of the coal,
And spuzzers and sorters fell in at the roll.

The light-infantry captains were Robin and Shack,
And the gallant big "benners" the victuals did sack;
Captain Green he commanded the Indigo troop,
These beer barrel chargers none with them can cope.

The Amazon army led on by Queen Bess,
Each feminine soldier so grand was her dress,
Though they chatted and pratted, 'twor pleasant to see
Them laughing and quaffing their hot rum and tea.

There was music to dainties and music to wine,
And for fear of invaders no hearts did repine ;
Although a dark cloud swept over the plain,
Yet our quarter was sheltered from famine and rain.

Drum-Major Ben Rushworth and Bandmaster Wright,
Drank to each other with pleasure that night ;
We'd full-flowing bumpers, we'd music and fun,
From the larder and cellar of Field-Marshall Lund.

One Private Tom Berry got into the hall,
When a big rump o' beef he made rather small ;
And Flintergill Billy of the Spuzzer's Brigade,
Got his beak in the barrel, and havoc he made.

The Field-Marshall declared, and his good lady too,
They ne'er were attacked with so pleasant a foe ;
With this all the clansmen gave them three cheers,
In return they saluted the bold Buchaneers.

The Benks o' the Aire.

I'T isn't the star of the evening that breetens,
    Wi' fairy-like leetness the owd Rivock ends,
Nor is it the bonny green fields up ta Steeton,
    Or the benks of the river while strolling wi' friends,
That tempts me to wander at twilight so lonely,
    And leave the gay feast for others to share ;
But O there's a charm, and a charm for me only,
    In a sweet little cot on the Benks o' the Aire.

How sweet and remote from all turmoil and danger,
   In that cot, wi' my Mary, I could pass the long years :
In friendship and peace lift the latch to a stranger,
   And chase off the anguish o' pale sorrow's tears.
We'd walk aght in t'morning when t'young sun wor
      shining,
   When t'birds hed awakened, an' t'lark soar'd i' t'air,
An' I'd watch its last beam, on my Mary reclining,
   From ahr dear little cot on the Benks o' the Aire.

Then we'd talk o' the past, when our loves wor forbidden,
   When fortune wor adverse, an' friends wod deny,
How ahr hearts wor still true, tho' the favours wor hidden
   Fra the charm of ahr life, the mild stare of ahr eye.
An' when age sall hev temper'd ahr warm glow o' feelin'
   Ahr loves should endure, an' still wod we share ;
For weal or in woe, or whativver cums stealin',
   We'd share in ahr cot on the Benks o' the Aire.

Then hasten, my Mary, the moments are flying,
   Let us catch the bright fugitives ere they depart ;
For O, thou knaws not what pleasures supplyin'
   Thy bonny soft image hes nah geen my heart.
The miser that wanders besides buried treasure,
   Wi' his eyes ever led to the spot in despair ;
How different to him is my rapture and pleasure
   Near the dear little cot on the Benks o' the Aire.

But sooin may the day come, if come it will ivver ;
   The breetest an' best to me ivver knawn,
When fate may ordain us no longer to sever,
   Then, sweet girl of my heart, I can call thee my own.
For dear unto me wor one moment beside thee,
   If it wor in the desert, Mary, wi' me ;
But sweeter an' fairer, whate'er betide thee,
   In ahr sweet little cot on the Benks o' the Aire.

In Memory of
J. W. PECKOVER,

Died July 10th, 1888.

HE was a man, an upright man
    As ever trod this mortal earth,
And now upon him back we scan,
    Whose greatest fault was honest mirth.

But never more his friends will see
    The smiling face and laughing eye,
Nor hear his jokes with heartfelt glee,
    Which made dull care before them fly.

Nor ever more the friend shall find,
    When labour lacks, the shake of hand
That oft was wont to leave behind
    What proved a Brother and a Friend.

In winter's bitter, biting frost,
    Or hail, or snow, or rain, or sleet,
The wretch upon life's tempest toss'd
    In him found shelter from the street.

The unemployed, the aged poor,
    The orphan child, the lame and blind,
The stranger never crossed his floor
    But what a friend in him did find.

But now the hand and heart are gone,
    Which were so noble, kind and true,
And now his friends, e'en every one,
    Are loth to bid a last adieu.

The Fugitive:
A Tale of Kersmas Time.

WE wor snugly set arahnd the hob,
 'Twor one wet Kersmas Eve,
Me an ahr Kate an' t'family,
 All happy I believe :
Ahr Kate hed Harry on her knee,
 An' I'd ahr little Ann,
When there com rappin' at the door
 A poor owd beggar man.

Sleet trickl'd dahn his hoary locks,
 That once no daht wor fair ;
His hollow cheeks wor deadly pale,
 His neck an' breast wor bare ;
His clooas, unworthy o' ther name,
 Wor ragg'd an' steepin' wet ;
His poor owd legs wor stockingless,
 An' badly shooed his feet.

" Come into t'haase," said t'wife to him,
 An' get thee up ta t'fire ;
Shoo then browt aght wur humble fare,
 T'wor what he did desire ;
And when he'd gotten what he thowt,
 An' his owd regs wor dry,
We ax'd what distance he hed come,
 An' thus he did reply :

" Awm a native of Cheviot Hills,
　　Some weary miles fra here ;
Where I like you this neet hev seen
　　Full monny a Kersmas cheer ;
I left my father's hahse when young,
　　Determined I wod rooam ;
An' like the prodigal of yore,
　　I'm mackin' tahrds my hooam.

" I soldier'd in the Punjaub lines,
　　On India's burning sand ;
An' nearly thirty years ago
　　I left my native land ;
Discipline bein' ta hard fer me,
　　My mind wor allus bent ;
So in an evil haar aw did
　　Desert my regiment.

" An' nivver sin' durst aw go see
　　My native hill an' glen,
Whear aw mud nah as weel hev been
　　The happiest of all men ;
But my blessin'—an' aw wish ye all
　　A merry Kersmas day ;
Fer me, I'll tak my poor owd bones,
　　On Cheviot Hills to lay."

" Aw cannot say," aw said to t'wife,
　　" Bud aw feel raather hurt ;
What thinks ta lass if tha lukes aght,
　　An' finds t'owd chap a shirt."

Shoo did an' all, an' stockings too;
    An' a tear stood in her ee;
An' in her face the stranger saw
    Real Yorkshire sympathy.

Ahr little Jim gav mommy a sigh
    When he hed heeard his tale,
An' spak o' some owd trousers,
    'At hung on t'chamber rail;
Then aght at door ahr Harry runs,
    An' back ageean he shogs,
He'd been in t'coit ta fetch a pair
    O' my owd ironed clogs.

"It must be fearful cowd ta neet
    Fer fowk 'at's aght o' t'door:
Give him yahr owd grey coit an' all,
    'At's thrawn on t'chamber floor:
An' then there's thy owd hat, said Kate,
    'At's pors'd so up an' dahn;
It will be better ner his awn,
    Tho' it's withaght a crahn."

So when we'd geen him what we cud
    (In fact afford to give),
We saw the tears come dahn the cheeks,
    O' t'poor owd fugitive;
He thank'd us ower an' ower ageean
    An' often he did pray,
'At t'barns wod nivver be like him;
    Then travell'd on his way.

The Feather'd Captive.

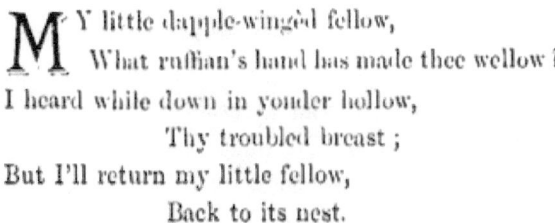

MY little dapple-winged fellow,
    What ruffian's hand has made thee wellow?
I heard while down in yonder hollow,
        Thy troubled breast ;
But I'll return my little fellow,
        Back to its nest.

Some ruffian's hand has set a snickle,
An' left thee in a bonny pickle ;
Whoe'er he be, I hope owd Nick will
        Rise his arm,
An' mak his heead an' ear-hoil tickle
        Wi' summat warm.

How glad am I that fate while roaming,
Where milk-white hawthorn's blossom's blooming,
Has sent my footsteps ere the gloaming
        Into this dell,
To stop some murdering hand fra dooming
        Thy bonny sel'.

For thou wur doomed my bird, for ever,
Fra all thy feather'd mates to sever ;
Were I not near thee to deliver
        Wi' my awn hand ;
Nor ever more thou'd skim the river,
        Or fallow'd land.

Thy feather'd friends, if thou has any ;
Tho' friends I fear there isn't many ;
But yet the dam for her, wi' Johnny,
      Will fret to-day,
And think her watter-wagtail bonny
      Has flown away.

Be not afraid, for not a feather
Fra off thy wing shall touch the heather,
For I will give thee altogether
      Sweet liberty !
And glad am I that I came hither,
      To set thee free.

Now wing thy flight my little rover,
Thy curs'd captivity is over,
And if thou crosses t'Straits of Dover
      To warmer spheres,
I hope that thou may live in clover,
      For years and years.

Perhaps, like thee—for fortune's fickle—
I may, myself, be caught i' t'snickle ;
And some kind hand that sees my pickle—
      Through saving thee—
May snatch me too fra death's grim shackle,
      And set me free.

Dame Europe's Lodging-House.

A BURLESQUE ON THE FRANCO-PRUSSIAN WAR.

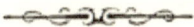

DAME Europe kept a Lodging-House,
  And she was fond of brass;
She took in public lodgers,
  Of every rank and class.

She'd French and German, Dutch and Swiss,
  And other nations too;
So poor old Mrs. Europe
  Had lots of work to do.

I cannot just now name her beds,
  Her number being so large:
But five she kept for deputies,
  Which she had in her charge.

So in this famous Lodging-House,
  John Bull he stood A1;
On him she always kept an eye,
  To see things rightly done.

And Master Louis was her next,
  And second, there's no doubt,
For when a little row took place,
  He always backed John out.

And in her house was Alex. Russ;
　　Oft him they eyed with fear;
For Alex. was a lazy hound,
　　And kept a Russian Bear.

Her fourth was a man of grace,
　　Who was for heaven bent;
His name was Pious William,
　　He read his Testament.

Her fifth, too, was a pious Knave,
　　And 'tis our firm belief,
He once did rob the Hungary Lads
　　Of hard-earned bread and beef.

These were Dame Europe's deputies,
　　In whom she put her trust,
To keep her Lodging-House at peace,
　　In case eruption burst.

For many a time a row took place,
　　While sharing out the scran;
But John and Louis soon stepp'd in,
　　And cleared the *padding can.*

Once, Alex. Russ's father, Nick,
　　A bit before he died,
Did roughly seize a little Turk,
　　And thought to warm his hide.

But John and Louis interfered,
　　Declaring it foul play;
And made old Nick remember it
　　Until his dying day.

Now all Dame Europe's deputies,
   They made themselves at home ;
And every lodger knew his bed,
   Likewise his sitting room.

They took great interest in their beds,
   And kept them very clean ;
Unlike some other *padding cans*,
   So dirty and so mean.

The best and choicest bed of all,
   Was occupied by Johnny ;
Because the Dame did favour him,
   He did collect her money.

And in a little bunk he lived,
   Seal'd up with oak, and tarr'd ;
He would not let a single one
   Come near within a yard.

A Jack-of-all-trades, too, was John,
   And aught he'd do for brass ;
And what he ever took in hand,
   No one could him surpass.

When tired of being shut in the bunk,
   Sometimes he went across,
To spend an hour with Master Loo,
   And they the wine would toss.

So many a happy day they spent,
   These lads, with one another ;
While every lodger in the house,
   Thought John was Louis' brother.

The Dame allowed John something nice,
  To get well in her rent,
Which every now and then i' t'bank,
  He put it on per cent.

And working very hard himself
  Amongst his tar and pitch ;
He soon accumulated wealth,
  That made him very rich.

Now Louis had a pleasant crib
  Which was admired by lots,
And being close by a window,
  He had some flower pots.

The next to Louis' bed was Will,
  The biggest Monitor
And though he did pretend a saint,
  He was as big a cur.

He loved to make them all believe
  He was opposed to strife,
And said he never caused a row,
  No, never in his life.

He was so fond of singing psalms,
  And he read his testament ;
That everybody was deceived
  When he was mischief bent.

He seldom passed a lodger's bed
  But what he took a glance,
Which made them every one suspect
  He'd rob if he'd a chance.

Now Louis had two flower pots
    He nourished with much care,
But little knew that Willie's eyes
    Were set upon the pair.

In one there grew an ALSACE ROSE,
    The other a LORRAINE,
And Willie vowed they once were his
    And must be his again.

He said his father once lodged there,
    And that the Dame did know
That Louis' predecessors once
    Had sneaked them in a row.

In Willie's council was a lad
    Well up to every quirk ;
To keep him out of mischief long,
    Dame Europe had her work.

To this smart youth Saint Willie
    Did whisper his desire,
One night as they sat smoking,
    Besides the kitchen fire—

" To get them flowers back again,"
    Said Bissy, very low,
" Meet Louis somewhere on the quiet,
    And try to cause a row.

But mind the other deputies
    Don't catch you on the hop,
For John and Joseph you must know
    Your little game would stop.

"For Joseph he has not forgot
   The day you warmed his rig ;
And christian Denmark still thinks on
   About his nice Slesvig."

"By your advice, my own Dear Mark,
   I have been guided on,
But what about that man i't'bunk ?"
   (Pointing o'er to John.)

"He's very plucky too is John,
   But yet he's very slow,
And perhaps he never may perceive
   Our scheme about the row.

"But not another word of this
   To anybody's ears,
The Dame she plays the list'ner,
   I have my doubts and fears.

"So let us go upstairs at once,
   I think it will be best,
And let us pray to Him above,
   Before we go to rest."

So with a pious countenance,
   His prayers as usual said,
But squinting round the room the while,
   He spied an empty bed.

"What a pity that these empty stocks
   Should be unoccupied ;
Do you think my little cousin, Mark,
   To them could be denied. ?"

"'Tis just the very thing," said Mark,
  "Your cousin, sir, and you,
Would carry out my scheme first-rate,
  One at each side of Loo."

The Dame being asked, did not object,
  If he could pay the rent,
And had a decent character,
  And Louis would consent.

" But I do object to this " says Loo,
  " And on this very ground,
Willie and his cousins, ma'am,
  They soon would me surround.

"They're nothing in my line at all
  They are so near a-kin,
And so if I consent to this,
  At once they'll hem me in."

" Oh ! you couldn't think it, Master Loo,
  That I should do you harm,
For don't I read my testament
  And don't I sing my psalm."

"'Tis all my eye," said Louis, " both
  Your testament and psalms ;
You use the dumbbells regular
  To strengthen up your arms.

"So take your poor relation off,
  You pious-looking prig,
And open out Kit Denmark's box,
  And give him back Slesvig."

" Come, come," says Mrs. Europe,
   " Let's have no bother here,
You're trying now to breed a row,
   At least it does appear."

Now Johnny hearing from the bunk
   What both of them did say,
He shouted out, " Now stop it, Will,
   Or else you'll rue the day."

" All right, friend John, I'm much obliged,
   You are my friend, I know,
And so my little cousin, sir,
   I'm willing to withdraw."

But Louis frothed at mouth with rage,
   Like one that was insane,
And said he'd make Bill promise him
   He'd not offend again.

" I'd promise no such thing," says Mark,
   " For that would hurt your pride,
Sing on and read your testament,
   Dame Europe's on your side."

" If I'd to promise aught like that,
   'Twould be against my mind ;
So take it right or take it wrong,
   I'll promise naught o' t'kind."

" Then I shall take and wallop thee
   Unless thou cuts thy stick ;
And drive thee to thy fatherland
   Before another week."

"Come on," cried Sanctimonius,
    And sending out his arm
He caught poor Louis on the nose,
    Then sung another psalm.

But Louis soon was on his pins,
    And used his fists a bit,
But he was fairly out of breath,
    And seldom ever hit.

And at the end of round the first,
    He got it fearful hot,
This was his baptism of fire
    If we mistake it not.

So Willie sent a letter home
    To mother old Augusta,
Telling her he'd thrashed poor Loo,
    And given him such a duster.

"What wonderful events," says he,
    "Has heaven brought about,
I'll fight the greatest pugilist
    That ever was brought out.

And if by divine Providence
    I get safe through this row,
Then I will sing 'My God, the spring
    From whom all blessings flow.' "

Meanwhile the other Monitors,
    Were standing looking on,
But none of them dare speak a word,
    But all stared straight at John.

"Ought not I to interfere?"
  Says Johnny to the rest;
But he was told by every one
  Neutrality was best.

"Neutral," growl'd John, "I hate the word,
  'Tis poison to my ear;
It's another word for cowardice,
  And makes me fit to swear.

"At any rate I can do this,
  My mind I will not mask,
I'll give poor Loo a little drop
  Out of my brandy flask.

"And give it up, poor Loo, my lad,
  You might as well give in,
You know that I have got no power;
  Besides, you did begin."

Then Louis rose, and looked at John,
  And spoke of days gone by
When he would not have seen his friend
  Have blackened Johnny's eye.

"And as for giving in, friend John,
  I'll do nothing of the sort;
Do you think I'll be a laughing-stock
  For everybody's sport."

This conversation that took place
  Made pious Willie grin,
And r ll John Bull to hold his noise,
  'Twas nought to do with him.

These words to John did make him stare,
    And finding to his shame,
That those were worse who did look on,
    Than those who played the game.

Now Mrs. Europe knew the facts
    Which had been going on,
And with her usual dignity,
    These words addressed to John :

" Now, Mr. Bull, pray answer me,—
    Why are you gaping here?
You are my famous deputy,
    Then why not interfere ?"

" Why," answered John, and made a bow,
    But yet was very shy,
" I was told to be a neutral, ma'am,
    And that's the reason why."

" That's just what you should not have done,
    Being in authority ;
Did I not place you in that bunk
    To think and act for me?

" Why any baby in the house
    Could not have done much worse,
But I fancy you've been holding back
    To save your private purse.

" Neutrality is as fine a word
    As ever a coward used,
The honour that I gave to you
    You shouldn't have abused."

The minor lodgers in the house,
  On hearing this, to John,
Began to whisper and to laugh,
  And call'd it famous fun.

At last a little urchin said,
  " Please ma'am I'd take my oath,
'At master John was neutral,
  And stuck up for them both."

"Stuck up for both, offended both,—
  Yes that is what you mean ?"
Continued Madame Europe,
  Then spoke to John again :

" Now I'll tell you what it is, John,
  We've long watch'd your career,
You take your fags' advice to save
  Your paltry sums a year.

" There's Bob and Bill, besides some more,
  That I call naught but scums,
They've got you fairly in between
  Their fingers and their thumbs.

" If such like men as Ben and Hugh
  This day your fags had been,
They would have saved both you and me
  This curs'd disgraceful scene.

" Instead of bein' half-clad and shod,
  As everybody knows,
You would have dared these rivals now
  To come to such like blows.

" There was a time in this house, John,
    If you put up your thumb,
The greatest blackguard tongue would stop
    As if they had been dumb.

" But not a one in this here house
    This moment cares a fig
For all you say or all you do,
    Although your purse be big."

" I couldn't hurt poor Louis, ma'am,
    Although he did begin ;
And then you see that Will and I
    Are very near akin.

" Beside, you see," said John again,
    " I let poor Louis sup ;
On both I use my ointment, and
    Their wounds I did bind up.

" Ah ! weel a day," then said the Dame,
    But was affected sore,
" I see you have some small excuse
    That you have done it for.

" I have some little hopes left yet
    That you may yet have sense,
To know your high position, John,
    Instead of saving pence.

" You yet will learn that duty, sir,
    Cannot be ignored,
However disagreeable when
    Placed before the board.

" And let me tell you he who shirks
   The responsibility
Of seeing right, is doing wrong,
   And earns humility.

" And 'tis an empty-headed dream,
   To boast of skill and power,
But dare not even interfere
   At this important hour.

" Better far confess at once
   You're not fit for your place,
Than have a name ' Heroic,' sir,
   Branded with disgrace.

" But I'll not say another word ;
   My deputies, to you ;
But hope you will a warning take,
   This moment from poor Loo.

" And hoping, John, your enemies
   May never have the chance
To see you paid for watching Will
   Thrash poor weak Louis France."

Charmin' Rebecca o' Riddlesden Hall.

ON Aire's bonny benks wi' her meadows so green,
There's an ancient owd hall to-day may be seen,
That wor built in the days of some owd feudal king,
Of whom the owd bards delighted to sing.
Tho' its splendour's now faded, its greatness was then
Known to its foemen as Red Lion's den ;
'Neath its armorial shield, an' hoary owd wall,
I now see Rebecca o' Riddlesden Hall.

Her majestic black eyes true beauty display,
Resemblin' truly the goddess of day ;
Her dark-flowin' ringlets, you'd think as they shone,
'At Venus hed fashion'd 'em after her awn.
For her tresses no ribbons nor trappins do bind,
But wantonly luxurious flow in the wind :
'Twod o' pleased the great Reubens or Turner to call,
To see sweet Rebecca o' Riddlesden Hall.

Like the tall mountain fir, she's as steady, I trow,
When zephyr-like winds do sighingly blow ;
The grove or the grotto when mild breezes move,
Are gentle Rebecca's sweet gales of love.
Her breath, where true wit so gracefully flows,
Has the beautiful scent of the pink an' the rose ;
There's no nymph from the East to Niagara's Fall,
To equal Rebecca o' Riddlesden Hall.

Her toe points the grahnd wi' sich beauty an' grace,
Nor varies a hair's-breadth, snd yu measure her pace :
An' when dress'd i' her gingham wi' white spots an' blue,
O then is Rebecca so pleasin' to view.
Wi' her gray Wolsey stockings by hersel knit an' spun,
An' a nice little apron, hieroglyphic'ly done :
It needs no rich velvets or Cashmere shawl,
To deck out Rebecca o' Riddlesden Hall.

Love, grace, an' beauty attend at her will ;
She wounds wi' a look, wi' a frown she can kill ;
The youths as they pass her, exclaim—" Woe is me !"
Who sees her must love her, who loves her must dee.
At Church on a Sabbath, owd men raise ther arms,
An' cry, " O, great heavens ! wor ivver sich charms ?"
While matrons an' maidens God's blessin' they call,
On the head of Rebecca o' Riddlesden Hall.

The City of "So be I's."

(A DREAM).

[It is said that when Giles Clumps, the South-downer,
first came to Keighley, the first question he asked his
fellow labourer was this, " What religion be th' master
here ?"   " A Liberal," was the answer; "So be I,"
says Giles.   " And what politics be th' master ?" asked
Giles again, " He's a Methody," was the reply; "So
be I," says Giles again, " I be a Methody too."   Now
do not imagine for a moment that Giles Clumps is the

only "So be I" in Keighley, for the whole town is full of "So be I's," and it is a well-known fact that if six long YELLOW chimneys were to turn BLUE to-morrow, there wouldn't be a Liberal in six hours in the city of "So be I's," with the exception of the old veteran SQUIRE LEACH.]

OH list to my dream, nor yet think it wrong,
  If I tell it in rhyme, or sing it in song;
For when I look back on the sights that were there,
I could almost, like Blondin, dance high in the air.

For when I reflect, my heart leaps with joy—
What I saw in my dream in old "So be I,"
For thousands were shouting on that pleasant day.
We are all "So be I's," hip, hip, hip hurrah!

And I took the first chance to ask what it meant,
Of the people who shouted, what was their intent,
When an elderly lady soon gave me the cue,
Of what was the matter and what was to do.

Six great millocrats, call them Whigs if you will,
The gods of our labour in workshop and mill:
Have all turned their colours from Yellow to Blue,
Which has caused this commotion the city all through.

Led on by the nose, like a bull in a band,
See how all the "So be I's" follow so grand,
The fag and the artist, the plebian also,
Have now chang'd their colour from yellow to blue,

There's twenty-eight thousand true " So be I's " here,
And there's not a Liberal amongst them I'll swear,
For the millocrats chieftains proclaimed it they say,
That all must turn Tories on this very day.

So upon the procession, I did my eyes fix,
Reviewing and skewing this wonderful six ;
They wore blue ribands so grand in their coats,
Singing " So be I " joskins come give us your votes.

The " So be I's " exerted each nerve and limb,
To follow their leaders and join in the swim ;
And I plainly could see, so I thought in my dream,
That the way through the world is to follow the stream.

For the faces of parsons were lit up so bright,
And the doctors they smiled with the greatest delight;
And a lawyer he vowed that he'd have a Blue gown,
For he'd been long enough a black Liberal clown.

Methought the Ranters, and Methodies too,
Independents and Quakers, and Baptists, were blue ;
And as I looked round me, lo ! what did I see,
A batch of Teetotallers had got on the spree.

But what I considered the best of the sport,
Took place in front of the old County Court ;
The Mayor and Ex-Mayor were dancing a jig,
With the County Court Judge in his gown and his wig.

Methought that the Draper and Hatter filed in,
Along with the Grocer, his nearest of kin ;
And I caught the Co-oper just in the neck,
In his hand were his divi. and new silver check.

Methought as I walked I sprang up so high,
That I really found out I was able to fly;
So backwards and forwards methought that I flew,
To the clubs of the town which I found were all Blue.

Till somehow or other, I got quite astray,
And over Cliffe Castle I wingéd my way,
Thinks I, there's some Foreign "So be I" geese
Have crossed o'er the Channel from Paris or Nice.

From thence I took wing, as blithe as a lark,
And crossed o'er the town to Jim Collingham's Park;
But ere I arrived at the end of my route,
A lightning conductor caught the tail of my coat.

I hung there suspended high up in the air,
Looking down on the mob in the wildest despair,
Imploring the "So be I's" to get me relief;
But they shouted "Stop there, you Liberal thief!"

I called on the de'il and invoked the skies,
To curse and set fire to all "So be I's;"
When all of a sudden I scratched at my head,
Awoke from my dream—found myself snug in bed.

Shoo's Deead an' Goan.

MY poor owd lass, an art ta goan,
    To thy long rest?
An' mun the cruel cold grave-stone
    Close ower thy breast?
An' art ta goan no more to see,
Exceptin' i' fond memory?
Yes, empty echo answers me—
    "Shoo's deead an' goan!"

I' vain the wafters o' the breeze
    Fan my hot brah,
I' vain the birds upon the trees,
    Sing sweetly nah;
I' vain the early rose-bud blaws,
I' vain wide Nature shows her cause,
Deeath thunders fro his greedy jaws—
    "Shoo's deead an' goan!"

There's more ner me 'at's sad bereft,
    I pity wun,
An' that's my lad—he's sadly left—
    My little John;
He wander's up an' dahn all t'day,
An' rarely hez a word to say,
Save murmuring (an' weel he may),
    "Shoo's deead an goan!"

Bud, Johnny lad, let's dry wer tears ;
         At t'least we'll try ;
Thy mother's safe wi' Him 'at hears
         T'poor orphan's sigh ;
Fer 'tis the lot o' t'human mack—
An' who can tell which next he'll tack ?
An' crying cannot bring her back ;
         "Shoo's dead an' goan !"

Ode to an Herring.

WEE silvery fish, who nobly braves
         The dangers o' the ocean waves
While monsters from the unknown caves
         Make thee their prey ;
Escaping which the human knaves
         On thee lig way.

No doubt thou was at first designed
To suit the palates o' mankind ;
Yet as I ponder now I find,
         Thy fame is gone :
Wee dainty dish thou art behind
         With every one.

I've seen the time thy silvery sheen
Wor welcome both at morn an' e'en,
Or any hour that's in between,
      Thy name wor good ;
But now by some considered mean
      For human food.

When peace and plenty's smiling brow,
And trade and commerce speed the plough ;
Thy friends that were not long ago,
      Such game they make ;
Thy epitaph is " soldier " now,
      Or " two-eyed stake."

When times are hard we're scant o' cash,
And famine hungry bellies lash,
And tripe and trollabobble's trash
      Begin to fail,
Asteead o' soups an' oxtail ash,
      Hail ! herring, hail !

Full monny a time it's made me groan,
To see thee stretched, despised, alone ;
While turned-up noses passed have gone,
      O' purse-proud men !
No friends, alas ! save some poor one
      Fra t'paddin can.

Whoe'er despise thee, let them know
The time may come when they may go
To some fish wife, and beg to know
      If they can buy
The friendship o' their vanquished foe,
      Wi' weeping eye.

To me naught could be better fun,
Than see a duke or noble don,
Or lord, or peer, or gentleman,
   In search o' thee :
And they were bidden to move on,
   Or go to t'sea.

Yet we'll sing thy praise, wee fish ;
To me thou art a dainty dish ;
For thee, 'tis true, I often wish.
   My little bloater ;
Either salted, cured, or shining fresh
   Fra yon great water.

If through thy pedigree we peep,
Philosophy from thee can keep,
An' I need not study deep,
   There's nothing foreign ;
For I, like thee, am sold too cheap,
   My little herring.

The World's Wheels.

How steady an' easy t'owd world's wheels wod go,
　　If t'folk wod be honest an' try to keep so;
An' at steead o' bein' hasty at ivvery whim,
Let us inquire before we condemn.

A man may do wrong an' scarce he to blame,
Or a woman be bad i' nowt bud her name;
Bud which on us owt ta say owt unto them,
Unless we inquire before we condemn.

If a Rose she sud flourish her sisters among,
It isn't to say her poor sister is wrong;
That blighted one there may be nipp'd in the stem,
So let us inquire before we condemn.

Yond vessel that tussels the ocean to plough,
While waves they are dashing and winds they do blow,
May be shatter'd asunder from stern unto stem,
So let us inquire before we condemn.

We are certain o' one thing an' that isn't two,
If we do nothing wrong we've nothing to rue;
Yet many a bright eye may be full to the brim,
So let us inquire before we condemn.

Then speak not so harshly—withdraw that rash word,
'Tis wrong to condemn till the story is heard;
If it worrant for summat sho might be a gem,
So let us inquire before we condemn.

English Church History.

Most respectfully dedicated to the Rev. F. D. CREMER,
St. ANDREW'S, Keighley, Oct. 25th, 1889.

DEAR reverend sir, excuse your humble servant,
 Whose heart you've made this very night to glow;
I thank you kindly, and my prayers most fervent
Will ever be, dear reverend sir, for you.

My ideas lacked for want of information,
 And glad am I to glean a little more,
About the Churches of our mighty nation,
 Whose chimes are heard on many a far-off shore.

My heart was moved, for I was much astounded,
 To view the many Churches of our land;
The life-like pictures of the saints who founded
 These ruins old, so wonderful and grand.

For oft I've wished, and often have I pondered,
 And longed to learn the history of our kirk;
How it was handed down to us I've wondered,
 And who were they that did this mighty work.

The veil's removed, and now my sight is clearer,
 Upon the sacred history of our isle;
For while I view these scenes it brings me nearer
 Unto the Church on which the angels smile.

Who would not shuffle off his worldly pleasures,
    For one short hour to bring before his sight,
The pictures of the great and mighty treasures—
    Our English Church, which brought the world to light.

Great Men dive deep down into wisdom's river—
    The poet, philosopher, and sage—
For wisdom's pearls, which showeth forth for ever,
    Nor waste their sweetness or grow dull with age.

Who would not walk through ruins old and hoary,
    And make each relic and persue his search ?
Who would not listen and applaud each story,
    Told of an ancient good and English Church ?

Each view so grand, mixed up with sacred singing,
    Of that old Church—I humbly call it mine,
For still my heart to it is ever clinging,
    And He who died for me in ancient Palestine.

Keighley Parish Church, 1891.

FROM A PHOTOGRAPH.

The Old Hand-Wool-Combers:

Lines written on the occasion of a Banquet given by
His Worship the Mayor (Ald. ICKRINGILL),
March 28th, 1891.

COME hither my muse and give me a start,
 And let me give praise to the one famous art ;
For it's not an M.P. or a Mayor that I toast, .
But the ancient Wool-comber, the Knight of the post.

In the brave days of old when I was a boy,
I went to the Comb Shop, my heart full of joy ;
Where I listened to stories and legends of old,
Which to me were more precious than silver or gold.

The old Comber would tell of his travels through life,
And where he had met with his darling old wife ;
And how he had stole her from her native vale,
To help him to pull the "old tup" by the "tail."

He would go through the tales of his youthful career,
An undaunted youth without dread or fear ;
He knew all the natives, the rich and the poor,
He knew every acre of mountain and moor.

He could make a sad tale of the wrongs of the State,
And tell where old England would be soon or late ;
How nations would rise, and monarch's would fall,
And tyrants would tremble and go to the wall.

He was very well read, though papers were dear,
But he got *Reynold's* newspaper year after year ;
It was bound to his bosom and he read it so keen,
While at times he fair hated a King or a Queen.

He was fairly dramatic, the stage he loved well,
The names of great actors and plays he would tell ;
And if that his notion it took the other way,
He could quote the Bible a night and a day.

Full of wit, full of mirth, he could give you a sting,
He could preach, he could pray, he could dance, he could sing;
He could play pitch and toss, he could jump, he could run,
He could shuffle the cards, he could handle a gun.

The old Constable knew him but let him alone,
Because he knew better than bother with "Joan";
For the lads of the Barracks and the Pinfold as well
Would all have been there at the sound of the bell.

Old Keighley was then but a very small town,
Yet she'd twelve hundred Combers that were very well known;
Hundreds have gone over the dark flowing burn,
Whence no traveller was ever yet known to return.

It reminds me again of the Donkey and pack
Which came from the hills bringing Wool on its back ;
And if the poor beast perchance had to bray
'Twere a true sign a Comber would die on that day.

The third day of the week, sometimes further on,
The old woman would seek the King's Arms for her son ;
And if she were told he had not been at all,
Would bounce over the green to the Hole-in-the-Wall.

Hi! those were fine times, especially the fairs,
When the Inns were kept open for dancing upstairs;
The Commercial, Lord Rodney, as well as the Crown
To the ancient Wool-comber were fairly well known.

But now we'll get back to the pot and the pad,
The fair it is over, the women are glad;
For now the Wool-comber his follies he sees,
And makes resolutions as staunch as you please.

For now he commences to work hard and late,
He is building a Castle on a phantom estate;
And he toils for a time but long hoggs make him sick,
Then he duffs, and his castle falls down, every brick.

When Winter comes in with its keen bitter blast,
And the poor rustic hind has to cope with the frost;
Yet the Comber was happy in village and town,
Though he knew that his calling was fast going down.

Oh yes, it was vanquished, the once noble art,
For science had bid it for ever depart;
Yet for thee old Comber fresh fields have arose,
That have found thee in victuals, in fuel, and clothes.

So many brave thanks to the Mayor of the town
Who has made the Wool-comber once more to be known;
Let us drink to the health of our worthy host,
The friend of the Comber, the Knight of the post.

T' Village Harem-Skarem.

IN a little cot so dreary,
    With eyes and forehead hot and bleary,
Sat a mother sad and weary,
      With her darling on her knee ;
Their humble fare at best was sparing
For the father he was shearing,
With his three brave sons of Erin,
      All down in the Fen countree.

All her Saxon neighbours leave her,
With her boy and demon fever,
The midnight watch—none to relieve her,
      Save a little Busy Bee :
He was called the Harem-Skarem,
Noisy as a drum-clock larum,
Yet his treasures he would share 'em,
     With his friend right merrily.

Every night and every morning,
With the day sometimes at dawning—
While lay mother, sick and swooning—
      To his dying mate went he :
Robbing his good Saxon mother,
Giving to his Celtic brother,
Who askèd for him and no other,
      Until his spirit it was free.

Saw the shroud and saw the coffin ;
Brought the pipes and brought the snuff in ;
This little noble-hearted ruffian,
      To the wake each night went he :

Sabbath morning he was ready,
Warn'd the bearers to be steady,
Taking Peter to his beddy,
    And a tear stood in his e'e.

Onward as the corpse was passing,
Ere the priest gave his last blessing,
Through the dingy crowd came pressing,
    The father and the brothers three ;
'Tis our mother—we will greet her ;
How is this that here we meet her ?
And without our little Peter,
    Who will solve this mystery ?

The Harem-Skarem interfered,
" Soon this corpse will be interred,
Come with us and see it buried,
    Out in yonder cemet'ry : "
Soon they knew the worst and pondered
Half-amazed and half-dumbfounded ;—
And returning home, they wondered
    Who their little friend could be !

Turning round to him they bowed,
Much they thanked him, much they owed ;
While the tears each cheek bedewed,
    Wish'd him all prosperity :
" Never mind," he said, " my brothers,
What I've done, do ye to others ;
We're all poor barns o' some poor mothers,"
    Said the little Busy Bee.

Come, Gi' us a Wag o' Thy Paw.

[T'West Riding o' Yorkshire is famed for different branches i' t'fine art line, bud t'music aw think licks t'lump, especially abaght Haworth an' Keighley. Nah Haworth wunce hed a famous singer; he wor considered one o' t'best i' Yorkshire in his time. It is said 'at he once walked fra Haworth to York i' one day, an' sung at an Oratorio at neet. He hed one fault, an' that wor just same as all t'other Haworth celebrities; he wod talk owd fashioned, an' that willant dew up i' London. Bud we hed monny a good singer beside him i' t'neighbourhood. Nah what is thur grander ner a lot o' local singers at Kersmas time chanting i' t'streets; it's ommost like bein' i' heaven, especially when you're warm i' bed. But there's another thing at's varry amusing abaght our local singers, when they meet together ther is some demi-semi-quavering, when ther's sharps, flats, an' naturals; —an' t'best ale an' crotchets mix'd, that's the time fer music.]

C OME, gi' us a wag o' thy paw, Jim Wreet,
   Come, gi' us a wag o' thy paw;
I knew thee when thy heead wor black,
  Bud nah it's white as snow;
A Merry Kersmas to thee, Jim,
  An' all thy kith an' kin;
An' hoping tha'll ha' monny more,
  For t'sake o' ould long sin'—
           Jim Wreet,
  For t'sake o' ould long sin'.

It's so monny year to-day, Jim Wreet,
  Sin owd Joe Constantine—
An' Daniel Acroyd, thee, an' me,
  An other friends o' thine,
Went up ta sing at Squire's house,
  Not a hauf-a-mile fra here ;
An' t'Squire made us welcome
  To his brown October beer—
                  Jim Wreet,
  To his brown October beer.

An' owd Joe Booth tha knew, Jim Wreet,
  'At kept the Old King's Arms ;
Whear all t'church singers used ta meet,
  When they hed sung ther Psalms ;
An' thee an' me amang 'em, Jim,
  Sometimes hev chang'd the string,
An' with a merry chorus join'd,
  We've made yon tavern ring,
                  Jim Wreet,
  We've made yon tavern ring.

But nearly three score years, Jim Wreet,
  Hev past away sin' then ;
Then Keighley in Appolo's Art,
  Could boast her trusty men ;
But music nah means money, Jim,
  An' that tha's sense to knaw ;
But just fer owd acquaintance sake.
  Come gi' us a wag o' thy paw,
                  Jim Wreet,
  Come gi' us a wag o' thy paw.

Full o' Doubts and Fears.

S WEET sing the birds in lowly strain,
 All mingled in their song;
For lovely Spring is here again,
 And Winter's cold is gone.

All things around seem filled with glee,
 And joy swells every breast;
The buds are peeping from each bush,
 Where soon the birds will rest.

The meadows now are fresh and green,
 The flowers are bursting forth,
And nature seems to us serene,
 And shows her sterling worth.

The lark soars high up in the air,
 We listen to his lays;
He knows no sorrow, no, nor care,
 Nor weariness o' days.

But man, though born o' noble birth,
 Assigned for higher spheres,
Walks his sad journey here on earth
 All full o' doubts and fears.

Behold How the Rivers!

BEHOLD how the rivers flow down to the sea,
Sending their treasures so careless and free ;
And to give their assistance each Spring doth arise,
Uplifting and singing my songs to the skies.

Find out the haunts o' the low human pest,
Give to the weary, the poor, and distress'd ;
What if ungrateful and thankless they be,
Think of the giver that gave unto thee.

Go travel the long lanes on misery's verge,
Find out their dark dens, and list to their dirge ;
Where want and famine, and by ourselves made,
Forgive our frail follies, and come to our aid.

Give to yon widow—thy gift is thrice blest,
For tho' she be silent, the harder she's press'd ;
A small bit o' help to the little she earns,
God blesses the giver to fatherless bairns.

'Neath the green grassy mounds i' yon little church-yard
An over-wrought genius there finds his reward ;
And marvel thee not, when I say unto thee,
Such are the givers that give unto me.

Then scatter thy mite like nature her rain,—
What if no birdie should chant thee a strain ;
What if no daisy should smile on the lea ;
The sweet honeysuckle will compensate thee.

For the day will soon come, if thou gives all thou may,
That thou mayest venture to give all away ;
Ere Nature again her balmy dews send,
Thou may have vanished my good giving friend.

Our Poor Little Factory Girls.

THEY are up in the morning right early,
　　They are up sometimes afore leet ;
I hear their clogs they are clamping,
　　As t'little things go dahn the street.

They are off in the morning right early,
　　With their baskets o' jock on their arm ;
The bell is ting-tonging, ting-tonging,
　　As they enter the mill in a swarm.

They are kapering backward and forward,
　　Their ends to keep up if they can ;
They are doing their utmost endeavours,
　　For fear o' the frown o' man.

Wi' fingers so nimble and supple,
　　They twist, an' they twine, an' they twirl,
Such walking, an' running, an' kneeling,
　　Does the wee little factory girl.

They are bouncing about like a shuttle,
　　They are kneeling an' rubbing the floor ;
While their wee little mates they are doffing,
　　Preparing the spindles for more.

Them two little things they are t'thickest,
　　They help one another 'tis plain :
They try to be t'best and t'quickest,
　　The smiles o' their master to gain.

And now from her ten hours' labour,
   Back to her cottage shoo shogs ;
Aw hear by the tramping an' singing,
   'Tis the factory girl in her clogs.

And at night when shoo's folded i' slumber,
   Shoo's dreaming o' noises and drawls :
Of all human toil under-rated,
   'Tis our poor little factory girl's.

Haworth Sharpness.

SAYS a wag to a porter i' Haworth one day,
   "Yahr not ower sharp ye drones o't'railway,
For fra Keighley to Haworth I've been oft enough,
But nivver a hawpenny I've paid ye begoff."

The porter replied, " I vary mitch daht it,
But I'll give a quart to hear all about it ;
For it looks plain to me tha cuddant pass t'snicket,
Baht tipping to t'porter thy pass or thy ticket."

" Tha'll write up to Derby an' then tha'll deceive me ";
" I willn't, this time," sed t'porter, " believe me " :
" Then aght wi thy brass, an' let us be knocking,
For I've walk'd it on foot, by t'Cross Roads an' t'
   Bocking."

Dear Harden.

DEAR Harden, the home o' my boyhood so dear,
  Thy wanderin' son sall thee ivver revere ;
Tho' years hev rolled ower sin thy village I left,
An' o' frends an' relations I now am bereft.

Yet thy hills they are pleasant, tho' rocky an' bare ;
Thy dowters are handsome, thy sons they are rare ;
When I walk thro' thy dells, by the clear running
      streams,
I think o' my boyhood an' innocent dreams.

No care o' this life then troubled my breast,
I wor like a young bird new fligged fra its nest ;
Wi' my dear little mates did I frolic and play,
Wal life's sweetest moments wor flying away.

As the dew kissed the daisies their portals to close,
At neet i' my bed I did sweetly repose ;
An' rose in the morning at Nature's command,
Till fra boyhood to manhood my frame did expand.

The faces that once were familiar to me,
Those that did laugh at my innocent glee ;
I fancy I see them, tho' now far away,
Or p'r'aps i' Bingley church-yard they may lay.

For since I've embarked on life's stormy seas,
My mind's like the billows that's nivver at ease ;
Yet I still hev a hope my last moments to crown—
In thee, dearest village, to lay myself down.

The Heroic Watchman of Calversyke Hill.

[This extraordinary "hero" either bore false witness against his neighbour, a poor artisan, or (taking his own word for it) saved the nation from great disaster and ruin by putting out a fire that no one saw but himself.]

WE'VE heard of great fires in city and town,
  And many disasters by fire are known ;
But surely this fire which I'm going to tell,
Was worse than Mount Etna, Vesuvius, or hell ;
For the great prophecy it no doubt would fulfil,
But for *l'heroic* watchman at Calversyke Hill.

This fire broke out in the night it was said,
While peaceful each villager slept in his bed :
And so greatly the flames did light up the skies,
That it took the big watchman all in surprise,
Yet great was the courage and undaunted the skill
Of the *heroic* watchman of Calversyke Hill.

He swore by his Maker, the flames rose so high,
That within a few yards, they reached to the sky ;
And so greatly they lighted up mountains and dales,
He could see into Ireland, Scotland and Wales !
And so easily the beaks did swallow his pill,
They fined the poor artist of Calversyke Hill.

Now, there's some foolish people are led to suppose,
It was by some shavings this fire first arose ;
But yet says our hero, " I greatly suspect,
This fire was caused by the grossest neglect ;
But I'm glad its put out, let it be as it will,"
Says the *heroic* watchman of Calversyke Hill.

He needed no witness to swear what he'd done,
Yet if he had wanted he could have had one ;
For one Tommy Twister, that never was there,
Saw the sparks from the chimney, as they flew in the air,
The greatest sized coal-pot no doubt they would fill,
Like the head of the *hero* of Calversyke Hill.

So many brave thanks to this *heroic* knave,
For thousands of lives no doubt he did save,
And but for this hero, disaster had spread,
And smothered the nation while sleeping in bed ;
But to save all his people it was the Lord's will,
Through the *heroic* watchman at Calversyke Hill.

So mind and be careful and put out your lights,
All ye with red noses in case they ignite,
Or perhaps from your bed you may have to leap,
In case this great watchman chances to sleep,
For as rumours are spread, he is fond of his gill,
Is the *heroic* watchman of Calversyke Hill.

The English "Cricketeer."

Lines written on the Keighley Cricket Club Bazaar
of 1869, and most respectfully dedicated to
the late William Luke Brown, Esq.

I SING not of grim-visaged war,
   Nor diplomatic rage,
But I shall string my harp in praise
   Of the worthies of our age.

They are a class of noble men,
   Whom England holds most dear.
Whose feats so grand adorn our land,
   Like the famous cricketeer?

The Ancient Greek his chariot ran,
   It was his Royal sport ;
The Roman gladiator fought
   To please the Royal Court.

The Spaniard with his javelin knife
   The wild bull's flesh he tears ;
But alack a-day ! what sports are they
   With our grand cricketeers.

And well old Keighley can be proud
   Of her famed sons to-day ;
Some of them are with us yet,
   While others are away.

Brave Brown ! brave Foulds and Waring,
   With good men in the rear,
And not forgetting Emmett,
   The brave old cricketeer.

Then while they have their Grand Bazaar,
    Pray let us rally round,
And give a hand to renovate
    Their well-loved cricket ground.

For well I wot both young and old,
    Will find from year to year,
More interest in the noble sport
    Of the grand old cricketeer.

The Mexican may throw his lance,
    The Scotchman put his stone,
With all the scientific skill
    Of muscle and of bone.

Give Switzerland her honour'd place
    With rifles and with spears,
But give to me our grand old sport,
    Our famous cricketeers.

Christmas Day.

SWEET lady, 'tis no troubadour,
  That sings so sweetly at your door,
To tell you of the joys in store,
        So grand and gay ;
But one that sings " Remember th' poor,
        'Tis Christmas Day."

Within some gloomy walls to-day
  Just cheer the looks of hoary gray,
And try to smooth their rugged way
        With cheerful glow ;
And cheer the widow's heart, I pray,
        Crushed down with woe.

O make the weary spent-up glad,
And cheer the orphan lass and lad ;
Make frailty's heart, so long, long sad,
        Your kindness feel ;
And make old crazy bones stark mad
        To dance a reel.

Then peace and plenty be your lot,
And may your deed ne'er be forgot,
That helps the widow in her cot,
        From out your store ;
Nor creed nor seed should matter not,
        The poor are poor.

Wi' Him I call my own.

THE branches o' the woodbine hide
   My little cottage wall,
An' though 'tis but a humble thatch,
   I envy not the hall.

The wooded hills before my eyes
   Are spread both far and wide ;
An' Nature's grandeur seems to dress,
   In all her lovely pride.

It is, indeed, a lovely spot,
   O' singing birds an' flowers ;
'Mid Nature's grandeur it is true,
   I pass away my hours.

Yet think not 'tis this lovely glen,
   So dear in all its charms ;
Its blossomed banks and rippled reels,
   Freed from the world's alarms.

For should love's magic change the scene,
   To trackless lands unknown,
'Twere Eden in the desert wild,
   Wi' him I call my own.

It isn't so wi' Me.

BRIGHT seem the days when I wor young,
  Fra thought, and care, and sorrow free;
As wild waves rippled i' the sun,
  Rolled gaily on, 'twor so wi' me.

More bright the flowers when I wor young,
  More sweet the birds sang on the tree;
While pleasure and contentment flung
  Her smiles on them, and so wi' me.

The naked truth I told when young,
  Though tempted wi' hypocrisy;
Though some embraced, from it I sprang,
  An' said it isn't so wi' me.

I saw the canting jibs when young,
  Of saintly, sulky misery;
Yet poked I melancholy's ribs,
  And said it isn't so wi' me.

Though monny a stone when I wor young,
  Is strong upon my memory—
I threw when young an' hed 'em flung;
  If they forgive, 'tis so wi' me.

Could money buy o' Nature's mart,
  Again our brightest days to see;
Ther's monny a wun wod pawn the shirt,
  Or else they'd buy—and so wi' me.

Yet after all I oft look back,
  Without a pang o' days gone past,
An' hope all t'wrong I did when young,
  May be forgi'n to me at last.

A New Divorce.

SAYS Pug o' Joan's, o' Haworth Brab,
   To Rodge, o' Wickin Crag—
" Ahr Nelly's tung's a yard too long,
   And by t'mess it can wag.

" It's hell at top o' t'earth wi' me,
   An' stand it I am forc'd ;
I'd give all t'brass 'at I possess,
   If I could get divorced."

Then answered Rodge, " I hev a dodge,
   As good a plan as any ;
A real divorce tha'll get of course—
   It willn't cost a penny."

" Then tell me what it is," says Pug,
   " I'm almost brocken-hearted,"
" Well, go to Keethlah Warkhase, lad,
   Where man an' wife are parted."

The Vision.

BLEST vision of departed worth,
   I see thee still, I see thee still ;
Thou art the shade of her that's gone,
   My Mary Hill, my Mary Hill.

My chamber in this silent hour,
   Were dark an' drear, were dark an' drear
But brighter far than Cynthia's beam,
   Now thou art here, now thou art here.

Wild nature in her grandeur had
   No charm for me, no charm for me ;
Did not the songsters chant thy name
   From every tree, from every tree.

Chaos would have come again,
   In worlds afar, in worlds afar ;
Could I not see my Mary's face,
   In every star, in every star.

Say when the messenger o' death,
   Shall bid me come, shall bid me come ;
Wilt thou be foremost in the van,
   To take me home, to take me home.

PRINTED FOR THE AUTHOR BY
JOHN OVEREND, COOK LANE, KEIGHLEY.